NUR

Life in orthopaedic Outpatients is never
dull for Nurse Imogen Brent, particularly
when she has to contend with the demanding Mr Roger Wemyss every day. But
when she is betrayed by her boyfriend,
Roger Wemyss is the only person to show
her any sympathy and Imogen is surprised
to find that there is another side to her
difficult boss . . .

NURSE IN DOUBT

BY

DENISE ROBERTSON

MILLS & BOON LIMITED
London · Sydney · Toronto

First published in Great Britain 1984
by Mills & Boon Limited, 15–16 Brook's Mews,
London W1A 1DR

© Denise Roberston 1984

Australian copyright 1984
Philippine copyright 1984

ISBN 0 263 74758 1

Set in 12 on 12½ pt Linotron Times
03–0784–39,000

*Photoset by Rowland Phototypesetting Ltd
Bury St Edmunds, Suffolk
Made and printed in Great Britain by
Richard Clay (The Chaucer Press) Ltd
Bungay, Suffolk*

CHAPTER ONE

IMOGEN lay in bed and contemplated the peach coloured ceiling of her room. 'It's Friday,' she thought. 'Beautiful Friday.' Not only was it Childrens' Day in Orthopaedic Outpatients but the Ear, Nose and Throat Department had a clinic too so there was always the chance that she might run across Nicky. She glanced at her bedside alarm and allowed herself two minutes to think about Nicky and the Orthopaedic Department and life in general, all of them things that gave her pleasure.

Imogen had always wanted to be a nurse, ever since she had discovered how satisfying it was to bandage and care for her toys. But her bank manager father had other ideas. 'I want you to join the bank, Imogen. It's a good, secure life . . . look how happy I've been in banking . . . you couldn't have a better profession.' So Imogen had dutifully joined the Bank after her A-levels and toiled over a computer for two years. At last, however, her father had seen she was pining and so she had come to Lanchester Royal with his blessing.

Her first year had lived up to all expectations but now that she was in her second year and working on Orthopaedic Outpatients life was

blissful. Especially now that she had Nicky!
She had fallen in love with Nicky Fleming,
House Surgeon to the Ear, Nose and Throat
Department, at first sight and he seemed to
return her love.

Thinking of him now she wriggled with
pleasure. With a bit of luck she would bump
into him several times in the course of the
morning and tonight they were going out for a
meal in the dimly lit Italian restaurant Nicky
favoured. Yes, life was sweet! There was only
one cloud on the horizon. Well, to be exact,
there were two. Mr Wemyss, the Orthopaedic
Consultant, was one and Sister Slater was
another. Except that Sister Slater was more
like a hurricane than a cloud. Just thinking
about her galvanised Imogen into action. She
swung her legs out of bed and began to get
ready to face the day.

She ran along the landing to the bathroom
she shared with five other nurses. Good! It was
empty. Her black hair was still in its night-time
plait and she held it out of the way as she stood
in the shower to soap her long, slim arms and
legs. One of these days she would have her hair
cut, but its natural curl would make it unruly
under her probationer's cap unless it was long
enough to be knotted at the nape of her neck.
When she was a staff nurse she could wear her
cap at a more rakish angle, but it would have to
wait until then.

When she had dried herself and slipped into

clean bra and pants, she unloosed her hair and surveyed herself in the mirror. Her dark eyes were too wide apart for conventional beauty but she had good cheekbones and, according to Nicholas Fleming Esq., MB, BS, an irresistible mouth. It curved into a smile now at the mere thought of Nicky and she was still smiling as she sped back to her room. Twenty minutes later she was groomed and dressed and queuing for breakfast.

'Imo . . . thank goodness I've found you.' It was Stella Roach, who had joined her in the queue. Stella was short and round with the pink cheeks of a country girl and worked in the Orthopaedic Clinic too.

'What is it now?' Imogen said with an air of mock-resignation as she collected her eggs on toast.

'Caps!' Stella said desperately. 'I've run out of clean caps and you know what the Dragon will do to me if I turn up like this.' Imogen looked at the bedraggled piece of linen perched on top of Stella's fair curls and nodded her head.

'I suppose I can find you a spare one . . . but I want it back! Don't forget! As soon as you get your laundry I want it back. I'm only doing it because I'll have to clear up the mess if the Dragon annihilates you.'

Stella settled herself into a corner seat with a sigh of relief. 'I knew you'd help me, Imo. You're so organised!'

Imogen remembered those words an hour later when she had finished rearranging the clinical trolley. She had thought it set out to perfection and then the Dragon, better known as Sister Slater, had ticked her off for having the PV tray on the left hand side instead of the right and ordered her to do the whole thing again. She was just finishing when Mr Wemyss swept into the clinic, the tails of his white coat flying behind him as usual.

'Not there, Nurse Brent. The PV tray always goes on the left hand side. And everyone—everyone but you, apparently—knows I like the sphygmomanometer on the top shelf, not the bottom. There are no X-ray Request forms in the rack and I don't see the knee-jerk hammer anywhere. Perhaps I am blind but as far as I can see it's not there!'

He was still grumbling when he moved into the first cubicle, swishing the curtain angrily aside. 'It's going to be one of those days' Imogen whispered to Stella, and it was only the thought of Nicky on the other side of the wall that kept her smiling.

The next moment Mr Wemyss moved backwards and closed the curtains with an angry rattle. 'I *am* going blind. Or else I'm losing my reason.' He turned to Imogen and fixed her with a steely blue eye. 'Is this Friday, Nurse Brent?' It was a statement, not a question, and Imogen did not reply. She knew from bitter experience that there was more to come. 'If it *is*

Friday am I correct in thinking that Fridays are devoted to children?'

Again Imogen stayed quiet as his voice rose. 'Well then, will someone tell me what a six foot man is doing lying on the examination couch in that cubicle?' Imogen felt her knees turn to water, then she lifted her chin and glared back at him.

'It *is* Friday, Mr Wemyss. And this is the Childrens' Clinic. I don't know what an adult male patient is doing in there but if you'll excuse me I'll find out.'

Mr Wemyss let out a snort and nodded his head. 'Very well, Nurse Brent. Get a move on. I don't want to be here all day.'

Imogen left the clinic and sought out Sister Slater in her office. Sister Slater had been at Lanchester Royal for as long as anyone could remember. 'She got left behind by the builders,' Stella was fond of saying and indeed Sister Slater did resemble stone. This morning she was sitting, immaculate as ever, writing up the large diary that stayed on her desk.

'Yes?' she said when Imogen appeared in the doorway. Sister Slater still wore the stiff collar and cuffs that most of the other sisters at the Royal had abandoned years ago, and she was the only sister in the hospital to retain the crisp bow under her chin. It acted as a storm warning. The angrier she got the more it crept up on one side or the other. At the moment, Imogen was pleased to note, it sat neatly under her chin.

'Yes?' she repeated. 'What is it Nurse? I haven't got all day.' Imogen drew a deep breath and launched into her tale. Before she was half-way through, Sister Slater was rising majestically from behind the desk and moving towards the door. 'I'll deal with this, Nurse. Get back to your patients.'

Imogen stayed a discreet yard behind Sister Slater on the way back to the clinic and once inside the doors she made herself scarce behind a screen.

'I understand you wish to know about the man in the first cubicle?' Sister Slater said. She was the one person in the whole hospital who was unafraid of Mr Wemyss. She had known him when he was a medical student working there in his vacation . . . or so the story went. She was certainly not putting up with any nonsense today. 'He's there because I put him there. His General Practitioner sent him in as an emergency. Far be it from me to judge the severity of his condition, but as he cannot put his foot to the ground his doctor's anxiety would seem to be justified and I would be grateful if you would see him before you begin your new patients.' Imogen was dying to see Mr Wemyss's face but the tone of his voice was conciliatory.

'If only someone had told me, Sister. You know I'm always willing to see referred emergencies. I like to be told what's going on, that's all. I don't ask a lot—a modicum of efficiency, some co-operation—that's all I'm asking.' His words were cut short by the crackle of Sister Slater's apron as she turned to the door.

'Thank you very much, Mr Wemyss. And now, if you'll excuse me.' A moment later she was gone and the clinic began. The emergency was a man of thirty complaining of low back pain which ran down his thigh and into his calf. Imogen knew enough about orthopaedics to know that his sciatic nerve was probably to blame and she was ready with the X-ray Request form when Mr Wemyss held out an impatient hand.

'He doesn't even say thank you,' she thought angrily, but she had to admit he was nice with the patients. She watched his hands move gently over the first child and marvelled at their skill. It was a small baby with congenital dislocation of the left hip. Mr Wemyss held the X-ray in front of the viewer and pursed his lips. Imogen held her breath. Would it be good news or bad? The baby's mother was looking anxious and Imogen smiled to reassure her. At last the surgeon nodded.

'Very nice. The acetabulum is coming round well.' He cupped his hand and put his other fist into it to demonstrate. 'I explained to you about the ball and socket, didn't I?' The mother nodded. She was looking at Mr

Wemyss adoringly and it was obvious she had complete trust in him. He put out a finger and let the baby grasp it.

'If we keep on with the frog-splint for a little longer, say another month, this chap will have a pair of perfect hip joints.' The baby was hanging on to the large forefinger with all its might and Mr Wemyss had to disentangle himself with his other hand. 'He's got a good grip, hasn't he?' he murmured to the mother, and they left her blushing with pride.

'If only he wasn't such an ogre,' Imogen confided to Stella at break. Stella rolled her blue eyes.

'You've got to admit he's dishy,' she said. Imogen looked up in surprise. Mr Wemyss was tall and broad and fair-haired, rather like a Viking marauder, with jutting eyebrows and a chin to match. Dishy was the last word she would use to describe him and she told Stella so.

'Your trouble is you've only got eyes for Nicky Fleming,' Stella said darkly. 'And we all know about Nicky.' Imogen bit her lip. She was tired of people hinting that Nicky was a philanderer. They couldn't know how nice he really was and she wasn't going to listen to gossip.

When they got back to the clinic there were some blood samples waiting to be taken to the Pathology Department. Imogen volunteered for the job in the hope that she might bump into Nicky in the corridor. Her luck was out.

She didn't see him on the way over to Path. and on the return journey she looked in vain for his tall figure. She arrived back at Out-patients to find Sister Slater in one of her rages. Imogen could tell from the set of the bow under her chin. It was tilting alarmingly and Imogen hoped she wasn't the cause of the trouble.

'Nurse Brent, do you know anything about the state of the linen cupboard?' Imogen's heart sank. She knew quite a lot about the state of the linen cupboard. Yesterday Stella had had one of her little accidents. She was trying to get some inspection cloths from the back of the shelf without unpacking the front. The inevitable result was that everything tumbled out on top of her. They were on their way to break and Stella had scooped everything up and pushed it back willy-nilly.

'I'll tidy it up as soon as we get back,' she had promised. Obviously she'd forgotten and Imogen blamed herself for not remembering. Stella's mind was like a revolving door. Ideas went in and out of it with alarming speed!

'I'm terribly sorry, Sister,' she said meekly. 'It got in a terrible muddle yesterday and I meant to tidy it up. I'll do it now if that's OK with you.' The moment the words had left her lips she realised her mistake.

'OK is not an expression we use in this clinic, Nurse Brent. Sloppy use of the language leads to sloppiness in other things, or so I believe. If you disagree with me perhaps you should be

working on some other department where
standards are less high.' It took five minutes of
grovelling to placate Sister Slater and another
fifteen to tidy the cupboard. And all the time
the morning was ticking away—the morning
when she might have bumped into Nicky and
snatched a few precious moments.

'I'm terribly sorry, Imo,' Stella said when
she joined her at the linen cupboard. 'I meant
to put it right. Honestly I did.' Stella's face was
so conscience-stricken that Imogen couldn't be
cross with her.

'Never mind, Stella. It's done now.' She was
closing the door when Mr Wemyss swept in.

'Am I supposed to have a nurse with me this
morning or am I supposed to soldier on alone?'
Imogen scuttled behind him into a cubicle and
tried to pacify the screaming two-year old who
lay on the couch. It took only minutes to
restore calm. The mother was persuaded to sit
in the chair by the couch, the little girl's eyes
were dried and Mr Wemyss could get on with
the job of examining her webbed fingers.

'This is a case of syndactaly,' he told Imogen,
pointing to the webs of skin that stretched from
one finger to another. 'And by the way, you're
good with children. Keep it up!'

Imogen was still trying to recover from the
shock of his compliment when he gathered up
his papers and took a final look around. 'Is that
it for this morning, then? Good. Thank you for
your help, Nurse. Good morning.' He zoomed

off as Sister Slater bore down on her with a handful of wet X-rays, still in their frames.

'Take these back to X-ray, Nurse Brent, and don't dawdle. I want this place cleared before you go to lunch.' Imogen sped along the corridor towards the X-ray Department, holding the wet X-rays away from the fold of her blue uniform dress. She was just about to push open the swing doors to the department when she heard Nicky's voice behind her. 'Hold on, Steve Ovett! I've been chasing you for the last five minutes.'

It was dark inside the X-ray Department and he drew her to one side. 'Still love me?' Imogen smiled, unwilling to indulge in love talk in such a place. Nicky put out a finger and traced the tip of her nose. 'Prim little Imogen. Never flirts on duty! You don't know what you're missing, darling. And think of me, slaving away in that dungeon of an ENT Department, dashing out in the hope of seeing you . . . and you fob me off! I'll have to look round and see if I can find someone more sympathetic. There's a new SEN on Mens' Surgical who's supposed to be rather hot stuff. Very forthcoming, or so they tell me.' Imogen stirred restlessly. She knew Nicky was only joking but she didn't like it when he talked like this. She didn't feel secure enough in his affection yet to be able to see the funny side of the joke.

'It's not that, Nicky. It's just that I'm in a hurry. If I don't get back the Dragon will murder me. You know what she's like.' Nicky nodded ruefully.

'Don't I just! Remind me to tell you about the time she caught me climbing over the back wall! She made me feel like a First Year at prep. school. OK, you'd better cut along. I'll see you tonight. I'm taking you to Nino's and then we can go back to the flat. James is on duty so we'll have the place to ourselves. See you.'

He planted a kiss on her temple and the next moment he was gone. Imogen moved towards the dark-room on winged feet. He loved her. He really loved her. And tonight they would be together for hours and hours.

Suddenly she felt a trickle of cold water running down her leg. Being with Nicky had affected her so much she had forgotten to hold the X-ray frames away from her dress. Now she had watery developer running down her legs. She handed the X-rays back to the dark-room technician and rubbed her leg with the hem of her dress.

'Are you working on Mr Wemyss's clinic?' the dark-room assistant said, glancing at the wet films as she pinned them up to dry. 'I think he's gorgeous . . . so macho. All the radiographers have a crush on him. You should see them falling over each other if he comes in here for something.' Imogen straightened up and made for the door.

'They must be mad. He's an overbearing, fussy, supercilious . . .' She was trying to choose between 'beast' and 'bear' when the technician's eyes flashed a warning. Imogen's eyes slid round to see Mr Wemyss's tall figure in the doorway, behind Mr Pilai the radiologist.

'Mr Wemyss wants to check on those laminectomy plates, Miss Dover. Do we have them ready?' Imogen felt her cheeks flame. Had they overheard? She forced herself to look up at him but he was staring straight ahead, his face expressionless, as though she didn't exist.

'Excuse me,' she said as she slipped past him, wondering as she did so why she felt so disturbed.

CHAPTER TWO

THE AFTERNOON seemed to drag. Under Sister Slater's eagle eye they had to check the surgical store, listing every item and cleaning the shelves. Then they checked the linen store. 'Some of this stuff came out of the Ark,' Stella whispered as they counted off linen draw-sheets and flannelette gowns. Most of the things they used now were disposable, to cut down on laundering, but Sister Slater still cherished her stocks from days gone by.

'The way she runs this place is feudal,' Stella said as they swung the doors shut at last and gathered up the lists.

'We're certainly treated like serfs,' Imogen agreed. 'All the same, Stella, she runs this place for the benefit of her patients. They come first as far as she's concerned.' Stella's blue eyes rolled in mock-agony. 'And we're a poor second. I'm glad you explained it—it'll be easier to bear now I know.'

At long last the hands of the clock reached five, but Stella and Imogen knew better than to appear at the clinic door. With some of the younger sisters you could announce the time and ask permission to go off duty. Not with Sister Slater! She preferred to seek you out and set you free, and if she found you toiling at your work the more likely she was to let you go.

'Lift that barge, tote that bale,' Stella hummed as they pretended to align the wheel-chairs along the clinic wall, and Imogen had to suppress a smile as the Dragon bore down on them.

By the time they came off duty and had some tea it was nearly six, which left Imogen with just enough time to get ready for her date with Nicky. As soon as she reached her room she stepped out of her uniform and dropped apron and cap into her laundry basket. Each pro-bationer at the Royal was issued with six caps and aprons. Laundry went twice a week and they were supposed to wear a clean one each day. Imogen found it easy enough to manage and usually had a spare or two to lend to Stella.

She hung her blue dress on a hanger and put it aside to air and then laid out a clean cap, apron and tights for the morning. More than once she had tried to persuade Stella to carry out this simple routine but it hadn't worked. One of these days she would have to sort Stella out but not tonight. Tonight she was going to be selfish!

She lay down on the floor, lifting her legs into the air, and wriggled closer to the wall until her legs were at right angles to her body She stayed like that while she counted to a hundred and twenty. A staff nurse had given her that tip in her first week on the wards. For the first time in her life she was on her feet for eight hours at a stretch, running here and there at everyone's beck and call. Her legs had become so tired and heavy towards the end of the day that she was almost limping as she came off duty. The kindly staff had advised her to stick her legs in the air for two minutes as soon as she got back to her room and, a little disbelieving, Imogen had tried it. It worked like a charm! Now, as she swung her legs down and got to her feet, she felt rejuvenated.

She gathered up sponge bag and towel and made her way along to the bathroom. It was empty and she slid home the bolt with a sigh of relief. She showered, using the precious perfumed soap that matched her talc and toilet water. It was rather expensive and she kept it for special occasions, so as soon as it reached her nostrils she felt special.

As she stepped into clean bra and pants she found she was singing 'I feel pretty'. The soundtrack of West Side Story was a favourite LP in the Recreation Room and she knew the words by heart. She did feel pretty tonight and the mirror told her she was looking her best. Small smiles were creeping round the corners of her mouth and try as she might she couldn't prevent them. She had meant to use a blusher on her normally pale cheeks but amazingly her face glowed with a gentle colour. 'It must be love,' she told her reflection and laughed aloud.

Suddenly she felt serious. It was strange, almost frightening, how Nicky had taken over her life. She had had other men in her life . . . at school, in the bank . . . men she had really liked to be with. But none of them had possessed such a hold over her. Nicky Fleming had the power to make or mar her day with a tilt of his head, one of his fabulous smiles. She clasped her hands in front of her and tried to analyse her feelings. Was it the glamour of his white coat that had got to her, the air of authority that even the most junior houseman seemed to acquire the moment he pushed a stethoscope into his pocket? No, it wasn't that. No one else on the Lanchester Royal's medical staff affected her that way. Only Nicky.

She pulled out the pins and shook her hair free so that it tumbled about her shoulders. The tight knot on her neck was fine when she was on duty but at night she loved the feel of hair about her shoulders. She brushed it free of tangles and then drew it off her forehead so that her straight dark brows and violet eyes showed to advantage. Then she patted moisturiser into her skin and applied a light make-up. When she'd finished she sprayed herself with perfume and stood back to take a critical look at herself. Yes, she would do. She stepped into her red wool dress and pulled up the zip. It was far from new but it was perfect for eating out, especially when she added a thin gold chain around her neck. She was humming as she let herself out of her room.

Stella was just outside, still in uniform dress and black tights. 'You look nice,' she said, wrinkling her nose appreciatively. 'And you smell nice too. Is it Nuit D'Or?' Imogen nodded as Stella slipped past her and flopped down on the bed.

'Yes . . . it's my precious Nuit D'Or and if you're a good girl I'll let you have one squirt before you go.' Stella groaned.

'All right, I can take a hint,' she said, struggling to her feet. Imogen bent down to adjust the strap of her black patent slingback shoe and then gave her friend a lavish spray of Nuit D'Or.

'Ta,' Stella said, moving towards the door. 'I'm going. I wouldn't dream of holding you up, not when you're going to meet the gorgeous Dr Fleming. It is Nicky Fleming you're meeting, isn't it? Or have you got some other hunk of manhood up your sleeve?'

Imogen picked up her bag and shawl. 'You should know by now that I never answer personal questions, not even when they're asked by nosy friends who should know better.'

She was still smiling at Stella's mortified expression when she tripped down the stairs and out into the open air. It was September and the light was fading, making the mellow red brick of the hospital glow in the last rays of the sun. I love this place, Imogen thought and shivered with contentment. The porter at the gate smiled and waved her through.

'Have a good time,' he said and she smiled in return. When she got into the street she could see Nicky's red sports car parked at the bottom of the road. He always picked her up a little way from the hospital.

'We don't want to set tongues wagging, do we?' he'd said when Imogen asked why. She wouldn't have minded the wagging tongues. To be known as Nicky's girl would be highly desirable as far as she was concerned. All the same she could see his point. The life of a junior houseman was difficult enough without gossip. Besides, the twin ogres of the Lanchester Royal, the matron and the administrator, were known to frown on relationships between junior medical staff and nurses.

The lordly consultants could do as they wished, Imogen supposed. Not that they made a habit of falling in love with nursing staff. Most of them were already married by the time they reached fellowship level and if not they had a glamorous girlfriend in tow, quite often a fellow doctor. Matron had an effective way of dealing with nurses who got entangled with medical staff. Nothing was said but they were quietly posted to Greenacres, the Royal's convalescent home on the outskirts of town. There were no resident medical staff at Greenacres and ward rounds were few and far between. Banishment to Greenacres was the ultimate

punishment and Imogen hoped she would
avoid it, at least for as long as Nicky was at
Lanchester Royal.

He leaned across to open the door as she
came abreast of the car. 'You look ravishing,'
he said as she slipped into the passenger seat
and the look in his eyes told her he meant what
he said. She accepted his proffered kiss on the
cheek and then settled back to enjoy the drive.
She loved to watch his slender brown hands on
the wheel, the competent way he handled gear
lever and hand brake. He had good hands.
Skilful hands. One day he would make a good
surgeon. She'd heard sister on Ward Nine say
so and everyone knew she was a good judge.

Before she came to Orthopaedic Outpatients she had worked on theatre and as she
watched the intricacies of the operating table
she came to see the different levels of expertise. All the surgeons at the Royal were competent but only a few had that special skill that set
them apart. Mr Wemyss was one, Mr Ryder,
the genito-urinary consultant was another.
And one day Nicky would be as good.

The next moment, or so it seemed, the little
red car was drawing up in the alley behind
Nino's Pizzeria and Nicky was helping her out.
'Mmmm,' he said, sniffing at Imogen's hair.
She knew what was coming next and she didn't
turn away. He kissed her cheek and then his
lips slid across to her mouth. 'You *are* lovely,
Imo. Cool and dark and mysterious like the

lady of the Sonnets.' Imogen didn't feel cool and dark and mysterious. She felt young and excited and decidedly weak at the knees. It was a relief when he took her arm and guided her into the welcoming depths of the restaurant.

The pizzeria was a favourite haunt of all the junior medical staff at the Royal and the waiters were only too willing to dance attention on them. They chose Spaghetti Carbonara and drank a carafe of Chianti. According to Nicky it was good but Imogen hardly tasted it. She was too busy watching the mobile face opposite—the quirk of his mouth when something pleased him, the way his eyes kept crinkling with laughter. One day, if she was lucky, she would be his wife. As they sipped their coffee she was indulging in a beautiful daydream in which she assisted Sir Nicholas Fleming in a major operation and then accompanied him to Buckingham Palace to receive the medal that was his just reward.

She was roused by Nicky's hand on hers. 'Wake up, dreamer. You were miles away. Are you tired? Did old Wemyss give you a hard time?' Imogen smiled and shook her head.

'No. Actually he was on his best behaviour today. He had an awful row with Sister Slater over an emergency she pushed onto his appointments list but she soon put him in his place. After that he was quite subdued . . . for him, that is.' Nicky smiled a knowing smile.

'Subdued was he? She must be mellowing

the old chap.' Curiosity brought Imogen alert!

'She? Who must be mellowing him? Sister Slater?' Nicky adopted the knowing look of someone who has information he knows will cause surprise.

'No. Not the Dragon! Although I'm sure she could make mincemeat of him if he chose. I mean the lovely Celia! Celia Graham, the Gynae Registrar. You know, the statuesque blonde with the good legs.' Imogen did know Dr Graham. She often passed her in the corridor and always admired her expensive clothes and impeccable grooming. Even her white coat seemed to have a couture air, she wore it with such flair.

The last time Imogen had seen her she had worn a yellow wool dress underneath her white coat, sashed with a bronze leather belt, and her bronze kid shoes must have cost the earth.

'They'd make a marvellous couple, I must admit,' Imogen said. Nicky nodded.

'Both blonde and Nordic, and they must be about the same age.'

Imogen had often wondered how old Mr Wemyss was. Sometimes he seemed like the Old Man of the Sea. At other times, when he was laughing with the children or sharing a joke with an elderly patient, he looked quite young. Suddenly she realised that it was his rank as Senior Consultant, Head of Department, that made him seem old, as though the acquiring of such prestige must have taken a lifetime.

'How old is he?' she said. Nicky pursed his lips.

'Early thirties. Something like that. I know he was one of the youngest candidates ever to get a fellowship. He was FRCS when he was thirty, I believe.' Imogen gave a little whistle of appreciation.

'Not bad!' Nicky's eyebrows shot up.

'Not bad? I'd like to think I'd do half as well. He must have worked like a slave, given up any fun or social life. It wouldn't do for me, I can tell you. However, it looks as though he's getting the lovely Celia, so he's not doing too badly.'

'Do you really think there's something in it—marriage, I mean?' Nicky shrugged.

'Who knows? He's a fly old bird with women. She's not the first to go after him and she probably won't be the last.' Imogen struggled with a vision of Mr Wemyss as the focus of so much feminine attention. It wasn't easy. He was so bad tempered!

'What do they see in him?' she said without thinking, and Nicky threw back his head and laughed aloud.

'Well, thirty thousand a year plus, for a start. Apart from which he's got family property, so they say, somewhere in Cornwall. And he's not a bad looking chap, Imo—super-fit and likely to stay that way. He's good company too, when he isn't breathing fire. Knows no end of jokes and tells them rather well!' Imogen was lost for words so she simply raised her brows to indicate her amazement. But Nicky had the bit between his teeth now and wouldn't give up the subject.

'He must be good at his job, Imo, because he's got where he is without pulling strings. You know how senior posts are given out . . . on the golf-course or over the port! Don't widen those great eyes of yours, Imo. That's the way life is in the medical world and you might as well realise it. It's not what you know, it's who you know. OK, you've got to have the initial expertise, I grant you that, but after that you have to sweet talk the people who count. Anyway, as I was saying, Roger Wemyss won't do that. Take me or leave me, that's his attitude. And obviously the powers that be prefer to take him.' Imogen regarded him with grave eyes.

'Is that how you'll play it, Nicky, when your turn comes?' Nicky smiled ruefully.

'Afraid not, kid. I shall wheel and deal for all I'm worth. When in Rome and all that. I mean to enjoy the fruits of success, Imo . . . whatever I have to do to get them!' Imogen felt unease stir within her at his words but she quelled it. When the time came he would change, she was sure of it.

The waiter came over then to offer more coffee and Nicky looked questioningly at Imogen. She shook her head. 'No thank you, I've had quite enough. It was a lovely meal. Thank you.' Nicky paid the bill and they left the restaurant hand in hand. Imogen could feel little prickles of excitement along her upper lip. They would get in the car and go back to Nicky's flat and be together for hours. Well, an hour and a half. She must be back at the home by eleven as she was on duty tomorrow. Nicky folded her tenderly into the car and then came round to the other side.

'I'm afraid I've got a bit of a disappointment for you, Imo darling,' he said as he slipped into his seat. Imogen felt her heart sink. Nicky was concentrating on the road, waiting to see when it was safe to edge out into the traffic.

'I know I said we'd go back to the flat but poor old Jimmy Edgerton has been on call seventy-two hours on the trot so I told him I'd look out for him for a few hours while he gets some sleep.' Imogen wanted to cry with disappointment but she knew she must not. Junior medical staff were always under pressure and had to help one another out.

'Never mind,' she said as cheerfully as she could. 'There'll be other times.' Nicky pulled up the car with a flourish, switched off the ignition and turned to face her.

'I knew you'd take it like that, Imo darling. You're such a good sport. That's why I love you so much. One of these days you're going to make a wonderful wife for a doctor!' Imogen sat very still, trying to work out whether or not that had been a proposal. Her heart told her it had been, her head said wait and see.

He leaned towards her, kissing her gently on the cheek, the nose, her trembling eyelids. 'Oh, Imo,' he whispered into her hair. 'Imo, Imo.' His lips travelled to her neck and lingered and she felt as though the thudding of her heart must surely communicate itself to him. She put up a hand and touched his hair, the smooth, shiny hair she loved so much. If she could have found words she would have spoken but they would not come. It didn't matter. As long as they could stay like this for ever nothing mattered.

The dream was shattered when Nicky straightened up. 'Must go, little Imo. I wish I didn't have to, but duty calls.' He sounded oddly cheerful, almost excited. As though he were moving off to a party rather than a spell of casualty duty. As the car moved off Imogen straightened her hair and tried to compose her face before she had to meet Stella's prying eyes. And then the car was pulling up at the usual place away from the hospital gates. She turned to Nicky, ready to slip once more into his arms, but he was already reaching across to open her door.

'Must rush, Imo darling. Can you manage?' The next moment she was out on the pavement and the red car was turning in the road and speeding away. Imogen had imagined he would drive through the gates and park at Casualty Reception. Instead he had driven in the opposite direction. She was still puzzling as she mounted the stairs to the home.

When she got upstairs Stella had just made coffee and Imogen accepted a cup gratefully.

'Nice night?' Stella said, and Imogen nodded enthusiastically.

'Marvellous,' she said.

Stella made a funny little face and then, seeing Imogen's eyes on her—'Good,' she said. 'I *am* pleased.' Imogen ignored the emphasis in Stella's voice but her heart sank. Stella was determined to say something and nothing Imogen could do would stop her.

'You *were* out with Nicky Fleming, weren't you?' Remembering Nicky's injunction not to gossip, Imogen smiled.

'Why do you ask?' she said.

There was silence for a moment and then Stella spoke. 'Because I heard he was meeting the staff nurse on Gynae tonight. She's on a split shift and due off at ten.' Imogen felt a flutter of agitation as she tried to raise her cup to her lips. The hot coffee stiffened her nerve.

'I wouldn't know anything about that, Stella. Sorry.' To her immense relief Stella seemed to accept her words and changed the subject to the topic of Maria Valent's radio, which had given up the ghost that night.

'We've fiddled with all the wires and it still won't work,' Stella sighed. Imogen sat gratefully drinking her coffee. For a moment she had been disturbed by Stella's announcement but now reason had reasserted itself. Hospitals were always rife with rumour and that was just another one.

When they'd finished their coffee they went their separate ways. Stella to tumble into bed, Imogen to go through her nightly routine of taking off her make-up and cleaning her teeth.

'Perhaps I *am* too organised,' she thought as she put away her sponge bag and towel and checked that everything was ready for the morning. 'Never mind,' her heart sang. 'Organised or not, Nicky loves you.'

As she slipped between the sheets she remembered what Nicky had told her about Mr Wemyss and Dr Graham. Had they been out together tonight? And had old Wemyss kissed Celia at the end of the evening as Nicky had kissed her? On the eyelids and the tip of the nose and the corners of the mouth? Suddenly she had a mental picture of the fierce Mr Wemyss kissing the immaculate Dr Graham and both of them in white coats with stethoscopes round their necks. It was too funny for words and she was still chuckling to herself as she drifted into sleep.

CHAPTER THREE

'I KNOW it's a bind but I've got to do casualty this weekend,' Nicky whispered when they met in the corridor on Thursday morning. 'But I promise—I swear—I'll be free next weekend and we'll spend it together. You'll be free too. We could go off somewhere for the whole two days.' Staff on Outpatients were free on Saturday and Sunday but Imogen wasn't too sure about going away somewhere with Nicky. She wanted to go, no doubt about that, but she wasn't sure she could handle it.

'Yes,' she said doubtfully. 'We could go away, couldn't we? Still, there's plenty of time to decide. If you're on duty this weekend I think I'll go home.'

Nicky smiled tenderly and brushed her cheek with his lips. 'You're a little home-bird, aren't you? Yes, you go home and have a nice restful weekend and I'll see you on Monday.'

So Imogen went home to be cossetted and fussed over. 'It's so nice to have you home, darling,' her mother said and Imogen could see that her father too was quietly pleased. Since Nicky had come into her life her days revolved around him. He was often on duty but usually he didn't tell her until the last moment and then it was too late to go home.

She spent Saturday afternoon in the woods near to her home, her dog, Benjie, gambolling at her heels. Benjie was overjoyed to have her back again, which gave her further cause for remorse. He ran for sticks, barked hysterically at rabbit holes and dug furiously around fallen tree trunks. It was peaceful in the wood with only the falling leaves for company, and Imogen enjoyed it to the full. If she was honest with herself she had to admit that the complications of her life at Lanchester Royal sometimes got her down. Wondering about Nicky, trying to keep quiet about her relationship with him, pandering to the whims of Mr Wemyss and being at the beck and call of the Dragon would have been enough without having to nurse patients and acquire nursing skills.

Nor was it any easier at tea-time. They settled around the fire, plates on their knees, and her mother poured tea. 'Now, darling, tell us all about the hospital. How is Stella . . . and that ogre of a sister you're so afraid of, is she behaving herself?' Imogen knew what was coming next. Her mother was moving in for the kill.

'And what about boyfriends? Do you go out much in the evenings?' Imogen would have liked to tell her parents about Nicky but something held her back. If they knew she was seeing him on a regular basis they would expect her to bring him home to be introduced. And in her heart-of-hearts she wasn't sure how Nicky would react to such an invitation. She could hear him now . . .

'Have a heart, Imo. You know I don't get much free time. Put them off for now, tell them anything. I'll come sometime, of course I'll come. I'd like to meet your family. But right now it's not on.' She was roused from her reverie by her father offering her the cake plate and to her relief the subject of boyfriends was dropped.

On Saturday night they played Monopoly and then watched an old Charles Boyer movie on TV.

'They don't make them like that any more,' her mother said, giving her father a meaningful look.

'Oh, I don't know about that,' Imogen said, exchanging glances with her father. He thought she was coming to his defence and smiled his gratitude but in reality she was thinking about Nicky. Loving Nicky, tender Nicky . . . darling Nicky with whom she would willingly spend the rest of her life. She was longing to tell her parents how marvellous he was but it must wait. Next time she came home perhaps, but not yet.

She came back to the Royal late on Sunday night, still full of roast beef and her mother's dreamy Yorkshire pudding. Stella was waiting anxiously to know if Imogen had an unlad-

dered pair of tights to spare and it was 11 p.m.
before Imogen tumbled into bed. She closed
her eyes, reflecting that tomorrow, with luck,
she would see Nicky—and then groaned as she
remembered it was Fracture Clinic day.

On Mondays all the patients suffering from
broken bones and ligment and muscle injuries
attended the Fracture Clinic. It was normally a
chaotic day with the waiting-room a jumble of
crutches and stretchers and people with arms
propped up on right-angled splints.

This particular Monday was worse than
usual. 'How much longer, Nurse?' the patients
asked wearily every time Imogen passed by.
Sister Slater's bow began to creep up on the
left and Imogen signalled a storm warning to
Stella, who was chatting animatedly to a young
Merchant Navy officer. He had been admitted
a few days before with a fractured clavicle and
discharged in a figure of eight bandage. She
was just in time. Stella made it back to the door
of the clinic seconds before the Dragon
erupted from her office.

'Nurse Roach, where have you been? Never
mind, just go and collect the wet films from
X-ray. Dr Singh can't get on until he gets
them.' She gave a searching look at the waiting-room clock and then looked back at Stella.

'I can take a hint,' Stella whispered as she
skipped past Imogen. 'If I'm not back double-
quick it's curtains!'

They had to take separate breaks so Imogen

didn't see Stella again until they met in the corridor an hour later.

'Can't stop,' she said, 'but did you see that divine Merchant Navy man? The fractured clavicle?' There was a note of caution in Imogen's voice when she replied. She had seen Stella fall for patients before and retire hurt. She didn't want to see it happen again.

'He's very nice, Stella. All the same you don't know much about him. He could be . . .' Stella didn't allow her to finish.

'He's not married, if that's what you're going to say. I checked his records. Besides, I know he's not. I can always tell. He doesn't rejoin his ship until the bandage comes off and it has to be readjusted daily. I hope Ram Singh keeps it on forever—that's probably how long it'll take him to ask me out.' She was suddenly downcast and then she brightened. 'Still, if he doesn't ask me I can always ask him.'

When Imogen followed Stella into the clinic she found Mr Wemyss battling manfully with a crowded and rather noisy roomful of people and set about restoring order. She darted in and out of the screens, helping people with buttons and armholes, hurrying them gently so she could put someone else in their place. There were never enough cubicles to go round on Fracture Clinic days. That was one reason why it was less smooth than other clinics.

People recovering from accidents were often slow on their feet, hampered by crutches or splints or painful joints. But they were also cheerful and optimistic, tolerating the confusion and helping one another whenever they could. Imogen usually wound up tired on Monday evenings, but with her faith in human nature restored.

Dr Singh, Orthopaedic Registrar, saw all the minor cases and did the plaster checks in the dressing clinic but Mr Wemyss liked to see all new cases and patients due for discharge.

'You must admit he's terribly conscientious,' Stella said, half-way through the morning. Imogen had just been subjected to a barrage of orders from Mr Wemyss and tried to produce a scowl.

'The operative word in that sentence is *terribly*,' she said darkly and pushed her wheelchair patient through the double doors.

As the morning went on the clinic began to clear.

'Are we near the end yet, Nurse Brent?' Mr Wemyss asked wearily. Imogen nodded.

'Two more behind the screens, another at X-ray and a stretcher-case outside, sir. I think that's all but I'll check with Sister if you like.'

Mr Wemyss held up a restraining hand. 'No thank you. I have troubles enough already. Let sleeping dogs lie. Ask Dr Singh if he can deal with the cases still to come in and I'll clear the screens.'

Imogen turned and went off to Dr Singh's clinic. She found him toiling away in a room full of patients but, in his usual good-natured way, he agreed to take on the stretcher-case and the check X-ray. Imogen went back to the clinic to find that Mr Wemyss had dealt with the two patients in the cubicles and they were struggling back into their clothes.

'He's letting me go,' an elderly lady confided to Imogen as she pulled on her felt hat. 'Says my hip's as good as new. It feels it too!' And she did an energetic dance to prove it.

'That's marvellous,' Imogen said, handing over the old lady's bag and stick.

'I won't need this much longer,' she said, flourishing the stick. 'He's fixed me up as good as new.' She leaned towards Imogen and fixed her with a roguish eye. 'Is he married? He's ever so handsome!' Imogen put a hand on the old lady's arm and urged her towards the door.

'No, he's not. But I'm afraid we'll have to hurry. More patients, you know.' The old lady formed her lips into an O of apology. 'Ooh, yes. I was forgetting. Righto, lead me to the door'.

Imogen ushered her out and then turned back to see if Mr Wemyss had any instructions for her. He was standing with case notes in his hand and Imogen recognised them as belonging to the old lady. He pointed to an X-ray he had just pinned in the viewer.

'You ought to take a look at this, Nurse. This lady had a fractured femur, quite a lot of separation. We decided to pin it and as you can

see we got perfect alignment. We used a Guttermann's pin to hold it in position and she
withstood the operation very well. She's got
good callus formation now, quite a textbook
case. I've discharged her and with a bit of luck
we won't see her again.'

Imogen looked attentively at the X-ray. She
could see the hairline crack that had once been
a fairly severe break, held now by a massive
pin. She tried to think of an intelligent question
to prove she was grateful to him for showing
her the film. 'Will you remove the pin at a later
date?' she said.

Mr Wemyss looked pleased at her interest
and launched into a lengthy discourse on fractured femora and the pros and cons of pinning.
Beneath the jutting eyebrows his blue eyes
gleamed like a fanatic.

'He really loves his work,' Imogen thought,
and tried to look engrossed. It wasn't hard to
look interested. He was doing his best to make
things clear to her and she found she was
understanding every word, which was more
than she could say about all Sister Tutor's
lectures. He had begun to discuss post-
traumatic arthritic changes when Imogen became aware that someone was standing behind
her. She looked round and met the cool grey
eyes of Dr Graham. Sensing that Imogen's
attention had wandered, Mr Wemyss hesitated
and looked around.

'I'm not interrupting, am I?' Dr Graham

said. Her voice was low and husky and Imogen
felt a small stab of envy. Dr Graham had a pale
blue tweed skirt and matching angora sweater
under her white coat and the single string of
pearls at her neck had the lustre of the real
thing. Her fair hair was drawn back from her
face and small pearl studs nestled in her ears.
She had a small gold fob watch pinned to her
lapel and a slim gold bracelet around her wrist.
She was smiling at Mr Wemyss, a smile that
revealed perfect teeth, and her whole appearance exuded glamour. Even the air was redo-
lent of expensive perfume.

Imogen sighed inwardly. She would like to
be like that, beautiful and self-possessed and,
yes, sexy. There was no getting away from it,
Dr Graham had sex-appeal and Imogen
sneaked a glance to see how Mr Wemyss was
reacting.

To her surprise he was staring fixedly at the
X-ray, leaning forward slightly to get a better
view.

'Ah, a Guttermann's,' Dr Graham said and
moved forward to stand beside him. 'It's a long
time since I saw anyone tackle one of those.
Not since my student days, I think. Perhaps I
could sit in on one of your theatre lists one day.
I'd hate to think I was getting rusty.' Mr
Wemyss made no reply and it was obvious that
Dr Graham expected one. She was looking up
at him from under lowered lashes and Imogen
decided it was time to clear out. Nicky was

right. Something was going on and she had no wish to play gooseberry.

She gathered up a pile of case-folders and was about to tiptoe out of the clinic when she saw Sister Slater through the glass porthole of the door. She was clearly in a furious temper. The bow of her cap was almost under her left ear and the whole thing was jerking angrily. If Imogen went out now she would be seized and given some terrible task to perform. Legend had it that Sister Slater had once set someone to cleaning out the sluice with a cotton bud and a bucket of Eusol. 'And I'm too tired for that,' Imogen moaned inwardly, thinking of her aching feet.

She looked back at the pair behind her. If Dr Graham moved any closer she would be nestling against Mr Wemyss. 'I'm caught between the devil and the deep blue sea,' Imogen thought. She hesitated for a further moment and then slipped into one of the empty cubicles. She could wait there until the coast was clear.

She stood behind the curtain, hugging the bundle of case notes against her chest. After a moment she turned and looked at herself in the mirror which hung in every cubicle so that patients could adjust their hair after dressing. Her cap was slightly awry and she put it straight. Her feet were still aching and she slipped off one of her shoes and rubbed her foot up and down her other calf. She wasn't

seeing Nicky tonight so she could have a blissful evening with her feet up.

She was wallowing in contemplation of the
delights ahead when she became aware of the
conversation on the other side of the screen.
Obviously Dr Graham believed herself alone
with Mr Wemyss. The intimate tones of her
voice told Imogen that!

'Actually, Roger, I came here with a devious
purpose,' she said playfully. She dropped her
voice. 'I wanted to ask you if you would like to
come to my place for dinner tonight. My
brother has sent a brace of grouse up from the
country and, as you know, cooking game is a
speciality of mine.' Mr Wemyss cleared his
throat.

'I'm afraid I'm not free this evening, Celia.
Otherwise, I'd have come with pleasure.' Dr
Graham gave a little moue of disappointment.

'Are you doing something terribly important? Couldn't you put it off?' Once more Mr
Wemyss cleared his throat.

'I'm afraid not. I'm writing a paper on compression fractures for the meeting next week
and tonight is my only free time. So, as I've just
said, I can't come.' Once more Dr Graham
sighed with disappointment.

'I *wish* you would. It's going to be a terribly
dreary evening for me on my own and I'm sure
your paper could wait. Anyway, you could
bring it with you and I'd help. You know you
only have to ask when you need help. Besides,

I have some awfully good claret I'd like you to
try. Do say you'll come.' Mr Wemyss's reply
was curt.

'I'm sorry. I can't. As I've just told you I
have to deliver my paper to the post-graduate
seminar next week and I must get it finished
tonight. If I don't, there won't be time for it to
be typed.' His words were stilted and his voice
had the rattle of a machine gun. Inside the
cubicle Imogen stiffened. She shouldn't be
hearing this sort of conversation! With all her
heart she wished she'd gone out and faced the
Dragon. Anything would have been better
than this!

She moved back until her legs encountered
the edge of the examination couch and sank
gratefully onto it. With a bit of luck they would
go in a minute and she could make her escape.
But Dr Graham was not the type to give up
easily.

'Oh, come on. To please me? You can work
tomorrow. I promise you I'll be a good girl and
let you get an early night. You'll work all the
better tomorrow for having had a relaxing
evening.'

Imogen felt the corners of her mouth creep
up in a rueful grin. Not even for the love of
Nicky would she plead and wheedle like that.
No man was worth it, not even the rich and
prestigious Mr Wemyss. She held her breath,
wondering what would be said next, and then
she realised she was still minus a shoe. If she

was trapped here much longer the Dragon would come looking for her. To be found lurking behind the screen would be bad enough but if she was found improperly dressed the sky would fall.

She put out a toe and tried to reach her shoe, lying a few feet away. She couldn't reach it. She wriggled a little further forward, listening against her will to the voices on the other side of the screen.

'Look, will you come for a couple of hours? Just to try the wine?' Imogen's toe touched the heel of her shoe, crept over the edge and began to pull the shoe towards her. And then it happened! She leaned too far forward, over-balanced and fell, and the case-folders cascaded around her.

The next moment the curtain of the cubicle was torn aside. 'What on earth is going on? What are you doing down there, Nurse Brent?' The tone of Mr Wemyss's voice was icy and Imogen felt a huge blush mounting in her cheeks. 'For heaven's sake get up and return those folders to their proper place. I'm off now. I'm late as it is. Good morning.' He gave a nod towards Imogen and another towards Dr Graham and turned on his heel. There was a gleam in his eyes which was either amusement or gratitude. Imogen couldn't be sure which but she was in no doubt about Dr Graham's expression.

As Mr Wemyss swept out of the clinic Celia

Graham regarded Imogen with pure hostility. 'So this is where you come to avoid work, Nurse. How enterprising of you. I must remember that.'

The next moment she had turned on her heel and pushed her way through the swing doors. Imogen clambered up from the floor and began to gather up the folders. It'll be a long time before she forgives me for this, she thought and it troubled her. Sooner or later she would have to work on the Gynae ward and now she had made an enemy.

CHAPTER FOUR

THE MORNING was hectic. Sister Slater sent her nurses scurrying here, there and everywhere and complained loudly about the time they took to carry out their tasks.

'When I get off duty tonight,' Stella said at break, 'I'm going to make a model of the Dragon and stud it with pins. I won't miss an inch. She's getting more impossible with every passing day.'

'She's not so bad,' Imogen said. 'Anyway, we've more important things to discuss than the Dragon. For instance, the dance. It's only two weeks away now, isn't it?' Lanchester Royal boasted a Staff Recreation Committee, composed of representatives from all grades of staff. They were responsible for organising sports and social activities, among them the dances which were held every three months. A local group provided the music and the charge-nurse on Mens' Surgical, who was a record buff, filled in at the interval.

'Are you going with Nicky?' Stella's eyes were on Imogen's face as she spoke. Ever since the subject of the dance came up Imogen had been dreading that question. Dreading it because she didn't know what answer to give. She and Nicky had talked about the dance several times and he had made it sound as though they would be together, but he had never actually asked her to be his partner and she was too proud to suggest it herself.

'I don't know,' she said as casually as she could. 'Even supposing we were, well, friends, and I'm not saying we are . . . you know what it's like. It doesn't do for medical and nursing staff to be too thick, not in front of Matron and the administrator.' Stella eyed her dubiously. It was obvious she knew Imogen was hedging, but mercifully she didn't press the matter.

'I wonder if old Wemyss will turn up with Dr Graham?' Imogen said, anxious to steer the conversation into safer waters. Stella groaned.

'Doesn't she make you sick? I mean, she's got the lot. Looks, figure, poise and money! Especially money. If I had her salary I'd be a knock-out, I promise you.' Imogen felt a sudden impulse to be fair to the absent Dr Graham.

'You can't put it all down to money, Stella. Yes, she does wear expensive clothes, but it's the way she wears them, a kind of flair, that makes her so outstanding.' Stella gave a grudging nod.

'I suppose you're right. It isn't doing her any good with our Roger, though. She's wasting her time, if you ask me.'

'How do you know that?' Imogen countered. 'Perhaps he's playing hard to get.' Stella leaned forward eagerly.

'I know all right. You should have heard Rafferty the other day.' Imogen raised her eyebrows. Rafferty was one of the porters and would have been well suited to a town crier's post. Stella saw Imogen's dubious expression and hastened to convince her.

'I know. I know he makes things up. But honestly, Imo, if you'd heard him you'd have known he was telling the truth. He said she waits outside in the courtyard, fiddling with her car keys, till old Wemyss comes out—and then she tries to chat him up!'

In spite of herself Imogen was intrigued. It was hard to believe that a senior registrar would lurk round corners waiting for a man, but since the conversation she had overheard the other day it just might be true. However, she wasn't going to tell Stella that. 'Perhaps she really was having trouble getting into her car. It happens, you know.'

Stella snorted. 'I'm not going to tell you anything else, Imo. You're too pure for words. But my money's on our Roger. She'll have to be clever to catch him napping.'

They were laughing about Rafferty and his stories as they arrived back from break. At that moment Sister Slater emerged from her room. The starched bow under her chin was squarely in place which meant all was well. She looked at them grimly for a moment and then her lips curved into a smile.

'I'm glad to see my nurses in such good humour in the middle of the morning. If you have so much energy it proves what I'm always saying, there's not enough work around here to keep you occupied.' Imogen knew what the Dragon was up to but Stella fell into the trap.

'Honestly, Sister, I'm worn out. The morning's been hectic and we've had three patients for replastering.' She held out her hands. 'I've still got plaster round my nails.' Imogen groaned inwardly. If only Stella would learn to keep her mouth shut! Sister Slater leaned forward and inspected Stella's finger tips.

'If you had scrubbed your hands efficiently, Nurse Roach, you wouldn't have that problem. Perhaps you'd better run along and do them now and give the sluice a clean while you're about it.' Every line of Stella's retreating figure conveyed reproach but Sister Slater was blind to it. 'And as for you, Nurse Brent, take these folders back to Records and then get back to your clinic.'

Sometimes the gods do answer prayers, Imogen decided as she skipped to the Medical Records Office. She had been longing for an excuse to get away from the Orthopaedic Clinic in the hope that she might bump into Nicky. She seemed to need him more with every day that passed. She shivered slightly at the mere thought of him and then she heard his voice behind her.

'Hold on, Imo. If you run along corridors like that you'll have Matron after you.' He drew alongside her and reached for her hand. She gave it reluctantly. Anyone might come round the corner at any moment! He turned her hand palm uppermost. 'Poor little Imo,' he said, and then he drew her hand up to his mouth and planted a kiss upon it. Imogen snatched her hand away.

'Nicky! Be careful.' He laughed and mimicked her anxious tones.

'*Nicky, be careful!* Wicked Nicky! Mustn't be naughty or heads will roll.' Imogen couldn't bear him when he was in this sort of mood.

'I've got to go, Nicky. You know what the Dragon will do to me if I dawdle. Besides, you're only teasing me.' He reached out a finger and drew it gently down her cheek.

'Yes, poor darling. I mustn't expose you to the fury of the Dragon. But I can't resist you when you look like that, so flustered and adorable.' As she went on her way her heart was pounding. 'Meet me tonight,' he had called after her, and she had nodded her head. Tonight! Eight hours from now she would be in the little red car with him. Delight welled up in her so fiercely that she had to pause outside Sister Slater's room and compose herself before she reported back from her errand.

It was more peaceful after lunch. The afternoon was set aside for attending to babies with congenital disorders and Imogen always enjoyed checking the tiny limbs and re-bandaging or splinting where it was needed. Nurses in training were not allowed to deal with the babies on their own and the Dragon's supervision was strict.

Today they were coping with a bilateral talipes equino varus in a baby of four weeks, a beautiful little boy with large blue eyes and a fluff of golden hair. He was perfect except for the fact that his feet turned down and inwards towards one another. He would have to spend time with them firmly bandaged in the correct position and supported by splints and eventually all would be well.

'May I hold him?' she asked his mother gently while Sister Slater was answering her phone. She always felt sorry for mothers of new babies, thrown suddenly into the hospital environment and worried about the outcome. 'He's coming on very well, isn't he?' she said, holding the baby close. The mother's tone was eager.

'Do you think so? I worry about him all the time.' Imogen shook her head.

'No need to. Before long his feet will be beautiful and, apart from regular check-ups, we'll be finished with you.' She looked down at the baby and kissed the velvet brow. 'You'll come back, David, won't you? Because I'm very fond of you. Did you know that?' There was a dry cough from behind her and she swung round to see Mr Wemyss standing in the doorway.

'I wouldn't wait too long for an answer, Nurse Brent. He's a little young to hold an intelligent conversation.' Imogen felt a flush rising in her cheeks. He really was an insufferable man, sneaking up on people with his sarcastic remarks. She was about to hand the baby back to its mother when he spoke again.

'No, don't do that. I want to have a look at him so you can hold him for me. You look much too nice together to be separated.' A moment later Sister Slater bustled in.

'Oh, you're here, Mr Wemyss. I've been ringing to remind you that you wanted to look at this patient.' There was a note of reproof in her voice, as though he should have waited by the phone until she told him to come.

Good for the Dragon, Imogen thought as she settled the baby in her arms for the examination. Considering the size of his hands, which were huge, the surgeon was surprisingly gentle with the baby. He unwrapped the tiny pink feet and allowed them to rest in the palm of his hand.

'There now,' he murmured, putting out his other hand to touch the baby's cheek. 'It's nice to feel the air on your feet, old chap, isn't it?' The baby gurgled appreciatively and Imogen, glancing at the mother, saw that she was looking adoringly at Mr Wemyss.

She should try working with him, Imogen thought sourly. Mr Wemyss was turning the small, deformed feet backwards and forwards, putting them into the correct position and then allowing them to return to their usual malformation.

'Yes,' he said slowly. 'They're coming along very well. Very well indeed.' He pushed back the baby's garments and prodded the tiny thighs. 'I think this one's going to be a rugger player,' he said thoughtfully. 'He's certainly got a good pair of legs.' The mother looked as though she were about to burst with pride and Imogen felt a grin spreading over her own face. To her intense annoyance Mr Wemyss looked up and caught her smiling. He almost grinned in return, but it was quickly subdued and he fell back to his task. A moment later he muttered his thanks and swept out of the clinic and Sister Slater began to re-apply the splints to the tiny feet.

Sister Slater let them off at five minutes to five and Stella's gasp of astonishment was audible. 'Any more of this and I'll be forced to believe she's human,' she said as she panted after Imogen. They were passing the door of the Histology Department, Imogen still ahead, when a large, white-coated figure swung through the doors. It was too late for Imogen to stop but she tried to take avoiding action. The trouble was the man moved sideways too! He put out his hands and caught her as they cannoned into one another. Her head came to rest beneath his chin and he held her for a second to steady her. There was a pleasant aroma of soap and tweed about him and the hands that held her were firm. She raised her head and looked into the quizzical face of Mr Wemyss.

'Are you running from or to the fire, Nurse Brent?' There was a mild reproof in his tone and Imogen bit her lip.

'I'm very sorry sir. I should have looked where I was going and I was going much too fast. I'm awfully sorry.' His hands fell to his sides and he twitched his coat into position.

'Never mind. No harm done. It's not the first time a nurse has run into me and no doubt it won't be the last.'

'He really is nice, you know,' Stella said fervently as they resumed their way along the corridor. 'Anyone else would have been really ratty with you.' Imogen was frowning.

'I can't stand the sarcastic way he treats people. I'd rather have had a good telling off than been treated like a naughty child.'

Stella laughed. 'I wish it had been me, that's all. I wouldn't mind being clutched to his manly chest, I can tell you. And he held on to you for *ages*.' Imogen was careful not to rise to the bait and simply hurried on.

When she got back to her room she took off her cap and apron and did her usual trick of lying with her feet in the air. When she swung her legs down she felt rejuvenated. She slipped into sweater and jeans and went down to tea.

'I forgot you were going out tonight,' Stella said as they ate.

Imogen stayed silent, determined not to let Nicky's name creep into the conversation. 'You know what people are like, Imo,' he had said, his lips against her hair. 'Give them an inch and they make a metre of it. I don't mean we should ignore one another or anything silly like that. It's just that we have to be discreet.' She had agreed with him but in her heart of hearts she had wished they didn't have to keep up a pretence. Anyway, half the hospital knew already or so it seemed.

'I suppose you're going out with Nicky Fleming,' Stella said, 'well don't say I didn't warn you.' Imogen was slow to anger and she was genuinely fond of Stella, but the words stung.

'Warn me about what, Stella? You're always hinting at things but you never back them up.' Conflicting emotions flitted across Stella's face and for a moment it looked as though she were about to speak but in the end she simply looked down at her plate. A moment later they were joined by two other nurses and there was a merciful change of conversation.

As soon as tea was over Imogen made her excuses and hurried back to her room. She slipped out of her jeans, wrapped herself in a towelling robe and padded along to the bathroom. To her horror the door was locked and there were faint wisps of steam creeping through the cracks in the frame. Someone was having a bath! A sudden trill of grand opera told her who was inside and she knocked gently.

'Hurry up, Maria. I've got an important date.' Maria Valent was a good-natured girl whose Italian parents kept an ice-cream shop in town. A moment later she emerged, her black hair curling round her face in damp tendrils.

'Sorry, Imo.' Imogen smiled her thanks and bolted inside hoping the hospital's notoriously erratic water system would not have slowed to an icy trickle.

By a quarter to seven she was ready. Much too early! She laid her jacket and bag on the bed and wandered over to the window. She would have to be patient for five more minutes or she would be waiting at the kerb when Nicky arrived. It wouldn't do to look too eager.

Outside, the red walls of Lanchester Royal glowed in the evening sun. Down below in the courtyard people were coming and going. Nurses in their uniforms, doctors with flying white coat-tails, the dark blue of an ambulance-man or the brown overall of a porter. Suddenly she saw a blur of vivid colour emerge from the shadowed doorway of the main block. It was Dr Graham, stunning in a geranium-pink suit. Even at a distance Imogen could see the gleam of gold in her ears and at her wrists.

There was no getting away from it, Dr Graham
was stunning. Any man who got her could
count himself lucky.

Imogen looked down at her own suit. Suddenly it looked old and shabby and dated and
she was seized with the desire to take it off. But
if she did there was only the red wool frock and
she couldn't wear that again, not yet anyway.

She was roused from her discontent by
curiosity. Dr Graham had crossed to her car, a
smart white Capri, but instead of opening the
door and slipping into the driving seat she was
standing there, looking over her shoulder.
After a moment she changed her briefcase to
the other side and then put a hand on the door
handle. She's going to get in, Imogen thought
but she was wrong. Dr Graham stood for a
moment and then walked around the car to the
passenger side and appeared to fiddle with the
door. Again she looked back at the hospital
entrance and suddenly Imogen remembered
what Stella had told her the day before. Of
course! She was lying in wait for old Wemyss!

As if to confirm Imogen's suspicions, the tall
figure of the orthopaedic consultant emerged
into the sunlight. Dr Graham had looked hastily away when she first saw him but now she did
a sudden, and to Imogen's eyes very artificial,
double-take. Mr Wemyss seemed not to notice
the elegant figure by the white car. He clutched
his briefcase against his chest and made for his
own car, a dark green Volvo estate parked in

the privileged area that was reserved for senior consultants. By now Imogen's nose was glued to the window-pane, her date with Nicky relegated to second place. What was going on down below was fascinating and not to be missed.

Dr Graham was galvanised by Mr Wemyss's seeming ignorance of her existence. She moved swiftly towards his car and stood there, one hand on the bonnet as though defying him to move off. He was stuck there, half in and half out of the driving seat and Imogen would have given a month's pay to hear the conversation. At last he eased in his long legs and put up a hand to grasp the door. Immediately Dr Graham put a slender white hand on top. If he was going to close the door he would have to trap her fingers inside. Imogen's lips pursed in a soundless whistle. The lovely doctor had it bad and no mistake.

The next moment the Volvo's engine roared to life, Dr Graham withdrew her hand, the door slammed shut and the big car purred away. What could he have said to make her relinquish her hold on the door? Dr Graham was walking slowly back towards the Capri and Imogen strained to see the expression on her face. But it was no use! The slim red figure slipped into the driving seat and suddenly Imogen remembered the time. Two minutes to seven! With a gasp she grabbed for her jacket and bag and raced for the door.

Nicky was sitting behind the driving wheel, one arm thrown nonchalantly over the back of the passenger seat. She had to tap on the window before he noticed her and then he leaned forward to open the door. She slipped into the seat and tried not to sound too breathless.

'We can't have the flat,' he said as they drove away. 'Jimmy is using it. As a matter of fact I'm not too pleased about it. However, we'll just have to make the best of it for tonight.'

'We could simply go for a drive,' Imogen said, 'somewhere in the country.' Nicky was nodding.

'Yes. I know a little pub just outside of Belton. We can pop in there for a drink.' She asked for lime and lemon and it came in a frosted glass. Nicky leaned across and put his hand on hers. 'I wish we could have gone to the flat tonight, Imo. We never seem to be alone, not really alone. What we really should do is get away together one weekend. I get awfully tired of being right on top of the hospital when I'm off duty. It means I'm too available and people can ring me about trivial affairs. We could go to the coast. There are plenty of small hotels there and you can always get a room, even at the last moment.'

Imogen kept her eyes fixed on her glass. She was afraid to look up and meet his gaze, even though she knew he wanted her to do so. He squeezed her hand.

'What's the matter, little mouse. Did I worry you when I said "room"? Of course I meant "rooms". You do trust me, Imo, don't you?' She nodded as vigorously as she could but she still couldn't meet his eye. She wasn't quite sure what she would see if she did. Amusement perhaps? Or mockery? Or even impatience? After all, she was being childish. She forced herself to look up and smile.

'I do trust you, Nicky. It's just that I've never been away before, not even for a weekend, unless it was with my parents. And I'm always nervous about new things. I can't help it.' He put out his other hand, unwound her fingers from her glass and clasped them in his own.

'Of course I understand, darling. And I'll be patient with you. Don't you realise that it's your shyness I can't resist. I love you for it, Imo. Never forget that.' The atmosphere between them had become intense and Imogen could feel herself trembling, so it was a relief when he released her hands and changed the conversation completely.

'Have you heard the latest about Roger Wemyss? He was giving a paper on compression fractures to the post-graduate seminar the other night and who should turn up but the lovely Celia. Apparently she sat herself down in the front row, looking knock-out as usual and applauding every word he said. Some of the chaps who were there said it was really obvious. Anyway, old Wemyss completely ignored her while he was delivering his lecture and then, when it was over, he picked up his papers and swept out. Didn't stay for the bun-fight or anything afterwards. Barney Colman was there and he told Jimmy it was quite embarrassing. She put a good face on it. Well, you know what she's like, very regal. But Barney said she was furious!'

Imogen was just about to tell him about the goings on in the courtyard, but some inner caution held her back. She didn't like Dr Graham and she had a horrid feeling that their paths would cross again before too long, but she was a senior member of staff and it didn't seem a good idea to speak about her too disrespectfully. It didn't seem too bad when she and Stella were gossiping together but this was different. Women should stick together. So she contented herself with raising her eyebrows and saying, 'I'm always a bit dubi-ous about these stories. They seem to grow as they pass from mouth to mouth.'

It was growing dark outside and the landlord was moving about, lighting lamps and drawing curtains over the leaded windows. They had another drink and then Nicky looked at his watch. 'It's five past ten,' he said. 'If we're going to get you back on time we should be making a move.'

They drove for a few miles along the road and then, without asking her, Nicky swung the car off the road and into the shadow of some trees. He switched off the engine and leaned back in his seat.

'That's better. I wish we were in the flat now with the stereo playing Vivaldi and a good bottle of wine.' Imogen wondered briefly why they couldn't have gone back to the flat anyway, whether or not Jimmy was there. There would have been nothing to stop them playing records and drinking wine together with Jimmy and his current girlfriend.

Her train of thought was interrupted as Nicky's arm moved smoothly around her shoulders. 'Come here, Imo. I want to feel you here beside me.' Again she felt that delicious tremor that only he could produce in her. She moved closer and turned her face into his shoulder but he put up a hand and cupped her chin.

'Don't hide your face from me, mouse. I know it's dark but I want to see those lovely eyes shining up at me.' Imogen looked up into his face but it was in shadow. And then his mouth came down on hers and he kissed her, a long lingering kiss. It lasted so long that she felt a faint panic and then his fingers were fumbling with the pins that held her hair and the next moment it had tumbled about her shoulders. He ran his fingers through it, gently at first and then tugging so that she had to restrain him.

'Sorry,' he said. 'Did I pull? Don't ever cut your hair, Imo. I would never forgive you if you did. It suits you. Sometimes I see you in the clinic and I want to reach out and pull it from under your cap so they can all see how beautiful it is. When we go away for that weekend I'll make you wear it like this all the time.'

At last Imogen moved away. 'I must go now, Nicky. You know what will happen if I'm late.' He leaned forward and switched on the ignition.

'You're right, of course. I can't get you into trouble with home sister.' He let out the clutch and the car moved smoothly away.

'I've had a lovely evening,' Imogen said as she unwound her long legs from the car and climbed out. Nicky leaned forward and smiled up at her.

'Same here, darling. But then I always enjoy myself with you. I wish we could meet this weekend but I've promised to cover for Barney. He's got something important on at home.' Imogen was disappointed but resigned. If you are in love with a doctor you must expect him to put duty first. She was hurrying towards the lighted hospital when she remembered they had not discussed the dance, and by then it was too late.

CHAPTER FIVE

IT WAS a relief when Monday came round and it was time for the Fracture Clinic. Stella could talk of little else but Clive, her Merchant Navy Officer, and his fractured clavicle.

'He'll need his collar and cuff adjusting so he'll have to come into the dressing clinic,' she said at breakfast. 'That means I'm sure to see him.' Imogen smiled.

'All right then, where's the panic? All you have to do is keep him waiting until he does make a pass. Or you could ask him to the dance.' Stella brightened.

'What a marvellous idea, Imo! Do you think I could?' To Imogen's relief she didn't wait for an answer and the conversation at the breakfast table turned to the dance.

'Will you wear your red dress?' Maria Valent asked. Imogen pulled a face.

'Not again. I've worn it at two out of the last three dances. No, I think I'm going to sport something new and daring and wildly expensive.' Stella's eyes sparkled.

'Like that divine thing Celia Graham had on last time, all drapes and bootlace straps?' Imogen hooted.

'You've got to be joking! At a rough guess

that dress cost sixty or seventy pounds. I'm planning to spend a fiver. I'm going to buy some material and make myself a dress!'

As they walked towards the Orthopaedic Department Imogen wondered what the morning would bring. She found the Fracture Clinic demanding but rewarding. It was nice to see people getting better. That was what nursing was all about. All the same, the hurly-burly in the waiting-room could get you down and if Stella was wafting about with only half of her mind on the job things could be chaotic.

Clive was already there in the waiting-room when they arrived. There was no sign of Sister Slater and both girls went over to speak to him. His face lit up at the sight of Stella. 'Do you think you'll get your discharge this morning?' she asked. He glanced at her and pulled a rueful face.

'Half of me hopes I will. Half of me hopes I won't. It's boring being ashore with nothing to do, but I don't know how I'll manage without this place when I get back to sea.' The look of rapture that appeared on Stella's face at this was almost comical.

Suddenly they heard the click of Sister Slater's heels on the tiled floor of the dressing room. 'It's all right. You hang on here and I'll head her off,' Imogen said and sped away. She pushed open the dressing room door to find Sister Slater only a yard away from her. 'Good morning, Sister,' she said, closing the doors behind her. As though she sensed that Imogen didn't want her to go out into the waiting-room, Sister Slater moved forward and looked through the porthole.

'Good morning, Nurse Brent. I see Nurse Roach is already ministering to her patients. Very creditable. Now, if all our patients were handsome navigating officers I feel I could safely retire and leave the conduct of the clinic to her. As it is, I fear I must continue to take charge. So if you will kindly step aside we will get on with the business of the day.'

Before Imogen could open her mouth the Dragon had swept out into the waiting-room and towards the star-struck pair. As she drew abreast of them she nodded a good-morning and went on her way, leaving Stella transfixed. Later on, when they were alone in the sluice, Imogen couldn't help but rub it home.

'I told you she knew everything that was going on. She's a downy old bird, that one. And really rather nice when you get to know her.'

Imogen just had time to check the trolley and make sure the appropriate case notes were ready in each cubicle when Mr Wemyss came in.

'Good morning. Come along then, Nurse. Let's get cracking!' His huge hand swept aside the curtain of the first cubicle and Imogen had no sooner joined him than he was holding out an impatient hand for the knee-jerk hammer.

She darted outside but to her horror it was not in its place on the trolley. And yet it had been here when she checked the lay-out!

'Come along, Nurse. Come along. I'm waiting!' Imogen bit her lip. If only she could have called back, 'Yes, I know you're waiting!' But junior nurses who talked back to senior consultants were never seen again. There was a limbo-land somewhere where matron kept them stoking fires, or so the story went.

'I'm awfully sorry, sir,' she said meekly. 'It was here a moment ago but it seems to have vanished.' The curtain moved back with an ominous rattle. Her heart sank as she saw the bristling eyebrows rise to new heights.

'Really? Vanished? You amaze me, Nurse Brent. Your knowledge of the metaphysical astounds me. So the knee-jerk hammer, simply an inanimate piece of metal, has metamorphosed into some other state of being! Or do you suspect telekinesis?'

If she had had the faintest idea what he was talking about Imogen might have given him an answer. As it was she could only stand there and fume. He was obviously waiting for an answer and there was a twitch of either annoyance or amusement playing around his mouth.

'Shall I go and look for it?' she said desperately. Anything to get out from under that steely gaze! The massive fair head shook slowly from side to side.

'I think not. I have lost a knee-jerk hammer. I couldn't bear to lose a nurse as well. If you will come back inside the cubicle, Nurse Brent, I will show you how to practice medicine without the aid of modern gadgets.'

Imogen stood there, lips compressed in anger, as he made a competent job of testing the patient's reflexes with the side of his hand. If she ever found out who had moved the knee-jerk hammer she would assassinate them! The clinic had been in progress for less than five minutes and already she had been treated to one of Mr Wemyss's bouts of sarcasm. Telekinesis indeed! She knew it was something to do with poltergeists but what it had to do with the knee-jerk hammer was beyond her. All the same, it *was* funny. She felt a smile creeping round her mouth and struggled to suppress it. She wouldn't give him the satisfaction of thinking she found him amusing!

She was shepherding the patient out of the cubicle when Stella breezed through the doors with the knee-jerk hammer in her hand. 'I thought you might be looking for this. I borrowed it for Dr Singh first thing.' Imogen looked over at the desk where Mr Wemyss was writing up the case notes. There was no point in Stella getting a dressing down too. But he appeared not to have heard and she contented herself with taking the hammer from Stella's outstretched hand. Stella cast a wary eye towards the consultant's desk and then moved closer.

'He hasn't asked me yet,' she said in conspiratorial tones. Imogen still couldn't trust herself to speak so she gave a sign that she must get on with her work and turned back to the patients. The next one was a comminuted fracture of the humerus, sustained in a fall from scaffolding. There were still faint traces of bruising about the man's face but his arm was comfortable inside the plaster and he answered Mr Wemyss's questions cheerfully enough.

'No, it don't hurt too bad, Doctor. I reckon I'm lucky to be alive so you won't get no complaints from me.' Mr Wemyss smiled.

'Well, that's the right spirit. But you will tell us if you begin to feel discomfort, won't you? Pain is nature's warning sign and we need to know when you feel it. That way we can be alert for something going wrong long before it becomes dangerous.' He really was terribly good-looking when he smiled, Imogen thought. The blue eyes widened and the stern mouth softened. He didn't look like the same man who had been mocking her a moment ago.

'I'd be better off if I was a patient,' she thought grimly as she turned away. All the same, the more she watched him the more she realised he was dedicated to his patients. 'I'd like to be like that,' she thought. 'I'd like to put my patients before everything.' As she moved about the clinic she wondered if that was what prevented a satisfactory relationship with Dr Graham. Perhaps there was no room for a woman in his life. It was a pity if that was true. Dr Graham was a fitting partner for an eminent surgeon. She would understand the demands of his work, she would be able to entertain for him and support him in the various social roles a surgeon was called upon to play. And she would look the part, no doubt about that!

And yet Imogen would have liked to see a little more warmth in Dr Graham's manner, a trace of softness in that immaculate exterior. 'Be honest,' she told herself. 'You'd like to see her with a ladder in her tights or smudged lipstick. So she would look like the rest of us.' She couldn't help smiling at the thought and with his usual knack of catching her off balance Mr Wemyss remarked upon it.

'I told you earlier that I found you amazing, Nurse Brent, but I must remark upon it once more. You've been driven off your feet so far and yet here you are, not a hair out of place and smiling into the bargain. Truly a remarkable performance!' For once Imogen was not going to let him get away with it!

'*Ah*,' she said archly, 'but I have such a good example before me.' He looked at her and smiled, teeth gleaming between his parted lips.

'Touché, Nurse Brent! Touché!' They waded through several more cases and then Mr Wemyss straightened up wearily and looked at his watch. 'Are you going to let me off the hook, Nurse Brent? I could do with a cup of that terrible brew matron insists on calling coffee.' Imogen could have let out a whoop of joy at the prospect of taking her own break but she was too well trained to show it. She contented herself with smiling graciously to show she appreciated his courtesy and stood back to let him leave the clinic. She had just finished refilling the cubicles ready for his return when Stella erupted into the clinic.

'He's done it, Imo! He's done it! He's actually asked me out. I'm so excited I don't think I can bear it. Did you know he's six feet tall? I asked him.' Her words were tumbling over one another and Imogen held up a hand for silence.

'Not another word until we get along to the canteen. If I don't get a coffee in a moment I'll pass out!' They asked Sister Slater's permission to go for their break and then hurried along the corridor, words still pouring out of Stella's mouth.

'I nearly died when he said it. I don't know how I'm going to live until tomorrow night. I'm just surviving on my nerves.' Imogen smiled grimly at this. Sometimes she felt Stella was living on *her* nerves! However, it was impossible to remain unmoved at the sight of Stella's happiness.

'Why don't we go to the Sports Centre tonight and have a game of badminton?' she said. 'That'll take your mind off your troubles.' The medical and nursing staff had permission to use the facilities at the nearby Sports Centre. Imogen had tried to get Stella to play before, but she had always refused. Today, however, she seized on the idea with enthusiasm.

'Ooh, yes, Imo. That's a marvellous idea. We'll play till we're tired out and then I'll get a good night's sleep.' They made their arrangements regarding times and the need to borrow a racquet for Stella and then sipped gratefully at their coffee.

'And now I must get back,' Imogen said. 'If old Wemyss gets back first and tells the Dragon I'm not at my post I'll be in Siberia tonight, never mind the Sports Centre.' She got back to the clinic a whisker ahead of the surgeon. A few moments later she was immersed in her work, the plans for the evening forgotten. The last patient was dealt with by one, then Mr Wemyss gave her his usual courteous thanks and departed. Imogen looked around at the disarray left by the morning's work and groaned. It was going to be a grim afternoon!

After lunch they set to and worked like slaves, too busy to exchange conversation. At last the clinic began to look its normal immaculate self and they breathed again.

'I've done the linen cupboard. I've done the sluice. I've dusted the desk and put things ready for tomorrow. I've checked the couches and the trays and now I'm going to hide in the stationery cupboard until two minutes to five, at which time I will reappear and accept dismissal!' Stella had just delivered this speech when the Dragon swept down upon them.

'Now then, Nurse Brent, Nurse Roach! Why is it I find you two hob-nobbing every time I come into this clinic? Is there nothing useful you can do? If you can't find something useful to occupy your time I'd better find something for you.' The two girls spoke in unison.

'No Sister. We still have a lot to do, thank you.' As the Dragon nodded her head and swung on her heel Imogen was sure she detected a gleam of amusement in the cold eyes— but with the Dragon you could never be sure!

When order was restored to the Dragon's satisfaction the hands of the clock showed ten to five and to their utter amazement she dismissed them with a wave of her hand. 'Run along now. I've had quite enough of you for one day. And be prompt in the morning.'

There was no court available when they got to the Sports Centre and they had to sit down and wait. They settled on the padded leather seats that lined the foyer and watched the people coming and going. There was an energetic and noisy game taking place on the adjoining squash court. Whoever was playing was ramming the balls home with force. You could hear them ricochet from wall to wall and occasionally one player or another would shout in triumph.

At last the court fell silent and the players emerged. To Imogen's surprise they were both familiar. Dr Singh was first, his dark face gleaming with pleasure and exertion. He was followed by the tall, muscular figure of Mr Wemyss, apparently not in the least out of breath or disturbed by his efforts. She would have been glad to greet Dr Singh, for whom she had a very soft spot, but she wasn't in the mood for another verbal sparring match with her boss. She averted her eyes and began to listen intently to what Stella was saying, hoping against hope that Stella wouldn't look up until the men had passed from sight. Stella was babbling on happily about the next evening when Imogen heard the unmistakable tones of Mr Wemyss behind her.

'Good evening, Nurse Brent, Nurse Roach. I didn't know this was a favourite haunt of yours.' His eye fell on their badminton racquets. 'So badminton is your game. Dr Singh and I have been playing squash. And an excellent game we had!' A rueful smile broke over the Indian's face.

'An excellent game, I agree. But I'm afraid you gave me a trouncing, sir.' Mr Wemyss had a white towel slung round his neck and he reached for the end of it and made a show of wiping his brow.

'I had to work damn hard to beat you, Ram. Don't be too modest.' He turned back to the girls and smiled. 'We're rather hot and dishevelled at the moment, I'm afraid, but if you give us time to shower and change we'd be happy to buy you a coffee.' He was smiling and relaxed, the broad throat brown and firm above the open neck of his white shirt. Out of the corner of her eye Imogen could see Stella's glowing face. Any moment now she would accept the invitation and plunge them both into half an hour of agony! Imogen rushed in:

'It's very kind of you, sir, but we came to play badminton and we don't have any time to spare.' She made her tone deliberately caustic so that Stella would take the hint and refrain from contradicting her. The surgeon's brow darkened but his voice remained even.

'As you please. I hope you enjoy your game. Goodnight.' Dr Singh looked unhappily from one to another and then hurried after the surgeon's retreating figure.

'You are so mean!' Stella said indignantly. 'In fact you're rude, Imo. And cruel. He never took his eyes off you once—and did you see those biceps!' Imogen had a suspicion that she had gone too far and it made her reply more acid than it might have been.

'I might have known he'd win. Poor Ram Singh is much shorter and lighter in weight. It wasn't a fair match.' Before Stella could answer the receptionist signalled their court was ready and they went in to play.

Stella was no match for Imogen but they had an enjoyable half hour keeping the shuttlecock in the air while Imogen got rid of her anger and resentment.

It was dark when they left but the moon was up and the walk back to the hospital was pleasant. The porter at the gates gave them a cheery wave from the safety of his lighted lodge and they hurried across the courtyard. Nursing staff were supposed to use a door at the far side but in the evenings they usually came in by the main door, which was nearer to their quarters. Everyone knew it was against the rules but no one seemed to mind.

Stella was ahead of Imogen as they mounted to the door, desperate to get to her room and rest her feet. She pushed the swing doors in her usual boisterous fashion and there was a startled gasp from the other side. The door swung back from Stella's hand and Imogen had to dart out of its way. She held it steady and then moved into the hallway.

Stella was stammering out an apology and stooping to pick some scattered papers from the floor. Dr Graham stood over her, her lips compressed into a thin line, her brows raised in anger. She wore a white poodlecoth coat over her violet dress and, as usual, she looked lovely.

'I'm terribly sorry,' Stella was saying, scrabbling at the papers and trying to hold on to her racquet and training shoes. Dr Graham swept her apologies aside.

'You shouldn't have come through that door at all, Nurse. You know nurses in training are not supposed to use that door. I assume you *do* know that?' Stella nodded dumbly. 'Then I ask you again, why were you charging through that door like a runaway elephant? If I hadn't been quick on my feet that door would have caught me full in the face.' Imogen gathered up the last of the papers and straightened up. She longed to come to Stella's defence but she didn't want to make matters worse. Dr Graham was making a great fuss over an unfortunate mishap but she would hardly take kindly to Imogen butting in.

'I'm waiting for an answer,' Dr Graham said. The normally ebullient Stella was silent and Imogen could stand it no longer.

'We're terribly sorry, Dr Graham. We should have been more careful coming through the door.' Before she could finish her sentence Dr Graham interrupted.

'You shouldn't have been coming through the door at all, Nurse. And being sorry would have been of very little use to me if I'd suffered a deviated septum. You seem to make a habit of being in the wrong place at the wrong time, Nurse Brent. You see, I know your name. I'm not in the habit of remembering the names of junior nurses but somehow I remember yours. If I find you out of place again I shall know exactly what to do about it!'

She put out a hand to the door and swept through, leaving the two girls aghast. 'What brought that on?' Stella asked after a moment. 'I was the one who nearly broke her nose but it was you she was mad with.' Imogen had a pretty good idea why she had aroused such rage but it wouldn't do to tell Stella about it. She shrugged.

'I don't know. Perhaps she felt she'd been hard enough on you and it was my turn.' They scuttled along the rest of the corridor to safety. They went into Stella's room and she whisked about, preparing coffee.

'Anyone else but her would have laughed it off,' Stella said as she scalded the cups. 'Still, I suppose we'll have to forgive her. It's probably frustration! She can't get her way with our Roger and she's taking it out on the poor overworked, underpaid nurses.' She heaved a theatrical sigh. 'I used to be like that. Bitter and twisted. And then a man wandered into my life clutching his fractured clavicle and since then I've been all sweetness and light!' Imogen giggled. 'You ought to try it,' Stella went on. 'Falling in love, I mean.'

'How do you know I'm not in love?' Imogen said impulsively. Stella's face clouded.

'That's what I'm afraid of, that you're in love with the wrong man.' Imogen groaned.

'Not again, Stella. Please!' Suddenly she put down her cup and stood up. 'You're completely wrong about Nicky. For some reason you're determined to misjudge him and I'm not going to sit here while you do it.'

They mumbled stilted goodbyes to one another and Imogen went back to her room.

She was angry with Stella but something else was on her mind. She had half agreed to go away for the weekend with Nicky. If she did she would have to lie to her parents. They wouldn't understand that it was a perfectly innocent expedition, a chance to get away from the stress of their working surroundings. So why did she feel so guilty about it? She was no nearer an answer when she put out the light and climbed into bed.

CHAPTER SIX

ON FRIDAY morning Imogen woke with her usual pleasant feeling of anticipation. Children's Clinic, she thought. Lovely!

'Clive comes in for a final check-up on Monday, doesn't he?' Imogen asked as they ate breakfast. Stella closed her eyes and screwed up her face.

'Don't talk about it! I can't bear it! I'll just have to speak to Ram Singh and get him to say there's no callus formation on the X-rays. How long do fractured clavicles take? Remember, his was a comminuted fracture.' Imogen pulled a grave face to match Stella's agonised one.

'Oh, I don't know. Surely he's better by now?' Stella sighed again.

'The trouble is half of me wants him to get better and the other half wants him to develop terrible complications. Something dangerous but not deadly, so that I could nurse him devotedly for a few months.' Imogen put down her cup.

'You wouldn't get to nurse him, remember. He'd go onto Mens' Medical and Miriam Blake would take care of him! Could you risk that?' Stella looked complacent.

'It wouldn't make any difference. He's not

the type to fall for a man-eater.' Imogen smiled but there had been an odd note in Stella's voice, as though she meant more than she was saying. A few moments later they were reporting for duty and there was no time to wonder what it might have been.

She carried the list of appointments into the clinic. Mr Wemyss had not yet arrived and she ran her eye over the list to see who was coming. She recognised several of the names, old friends who came regularly. Among them was Alexander Dodd and Imogen winced at the prospect. Personally, she had a very soft spot for Alexander but he was quite capable of reducing the clinic to chaos. A small boy, his legs in calipers and walking with sticks, he fought every inch of the way. Imogen was sure he felt afraid of the hospital atmosphere and became dictatorial and unpleasant to cover up his fear. Other people felt he was simply a little trouble-maker who needed firm handling.

Several times Sister Slater had been called in to subdue Alexander and comfort his harassed mother but Imogen was sure that if she could only get through to the child she could get him to co-operate. She made a mental note to have a word with him in the waiting room before he came into the clinic so that he would feel more at home when he finally saw the surgeon.

She finished reading the list as the clinic doors opened and Mr Wemyss appeared. He swept up to the desk and picked up the list. He

wore a crisp blue shirt and dark blue tie that set
off his eyes and there was a well-scrubbed glow
of health and vitality about him. Grudgingly
Imogen admitted to herself that he was a handsome man. Still, handsome is as handsome
does she thought. He looked up from the list
and caught her eye.

'Good morning, Nurse. I see we have a full
complement of rogues and vagabonds this
morning. You'd better wheel in the first one.'
The first patient was an angelic little girl who'd
been born with a congenitally dislocated hip.
She had worn a frog plaster from birth until she
was a year old. Now, at four and a half, she
came back for twice-yearly check-ups. Today
she pirouetted up and down the clinic, showing
off her progress. Obviously she regarded Mr
Wemyss as a close, personal friend. When she
had shown how well she could walk she came
close to his knee and looked up into his face. 'I
can dance, you know,' she said solemnly. He
raised his eyebrows, unsmiling.

'Are you any good?' he said sternly. The
little girl's face was equally serious.

'Yes,' she said firmly.

The surgeon nodded. 'I thought you would
be.'

'Shall I show you?' she asked. He looked at
her in surprise.

'Of course,' he said. 'You didn't think I'd let
you go without showing me, did you?'

The press of patients outside the door, the

routine of the clinic was forgotten. Doctor, nurse and parents all sat and watched as a small figure tapped between desks and trolleys and couches. When she came to a halt in a sweeping curtsey they applauded to a man, and suddenly Imogen felt a constriction in her throat. The more she got to know Mr Wemyss the more she admired him. He seemed to care totally for his patients, not only for their bodies but for their spirits. The little girl departed, radiant, and the next patient took his turn at the desk.

He had suffered a particularly bad fracture of his radius and now there were complications with the epiphysis, the growing end of the bone, so he had become an orthopaedic case. Mr Wemyss was examining the arm with care, asking the boy to grip his fingers and make a fist. After a while he looked up at the boy and smiled.

'It's coming along well, old chap. However, I'm not quite sure it's going to make the grade all on its own. What I'd like to do is go in there later and make sure you have a good, sturdy forearm for that train you want to drive.' The boy nodded. Obviously he was content with whatever Mr. Wemyss might decide. The surgeon looked at the mother.

'It may not be necessary. We're keeping a very careful eye on the epiphyseal development. If we're lucky we won't need to do anything. But if not . . .' As the child rose to leave he was smiling cheerfully and once more

Imogen was impressed. She might feel the sting of his sarcasm but with his patients he was always gentle.

Suddenly there was a crash and the clinic door was flung back on its hinges. In the doorway stood the small, vengeful figure of Alexander Dodd. He lifted one of his sticks and pointed it accusingly at Mr Wemyss. 'I'm not staying in! I told you that last time. No more coming in! I don't care what you say about it, I'm not coming in. I'll come here and you can do things but I'm not going back in the ward.'

Imogen held her breath. Adult patients wouldn't get away with a speech like that, let alone an eight year old boy. Mr Wemyss sat back in his chair and surveyed the threatening figure, less threatening now that there was a solitary tear in his eye. 'Why don't you come over here and sit down and we'll talk about it,' he said equably. 'You know it's sometimes necessary for you to be admitted. Until we get those legs of yours into shape you need treatment. I don't know if you'll need to be admitted today but even if I suggest it you can always say no. I've told you that before, Alex. You're master of your own fate. You and your parents. I only make suggestions. It's up to you to accept or reject them. I think I can make you better eventually and I hope you're going to let me try.' Alexander was wavering. He advanced a few steps and looked warily at Mr Wemyss.

'I don't have to come in if I don't want to?'
Mr Wemyss nodded. 'Well, I don't want to so
that's settled.' Alexander moved to the desk.
Doctor and patient eyed each other for a moment and then Mr Wemyss ordered X-rays.
Imogen made out the form and shepherded the
little boy out of the clinic. Mrs Dodd, harassed
as usual, brought up the rear. Imogen pointed
them in the direction of the X-ray Department
and then returned to the clinic.

Alexander seemed to have brought them
luck. The next half-dozen patients were easy
and the list began to bear an impressive num-
ber of ticks.

'Do you think you could arrange a hiatus,
Nurse Brent?' Mr Wemyss enquired as they
emerged from a cubicle. Imogen nodded.

'If you see one more desk case and a cubicle,
sir, that should leave you free for twenty minutes or so. After that we have the patients
coming back from X-ray and some bi-valved
plasters for inspection.' Mr Wemyss rubbed his
hands together.

'Splendid. Let's get on with it, I'm desperate
for a cup of coffee.' They rattled through the
waiting cases and then he went off, promising
to return promptly. Imogen checked that
things were in order for his return and then
went off for her own break. Poor Stella was up
to her eyes in rebandaging and splinting and
Imogen had to set off alone. She stepped into
the corridor, hoping to hear Nicky's voice or

have him appear. But she was on her way back to duty before she met him.

'Hold on! Surely you can spare time for a poor but honest Bachelor of Medicine?' In spite of herself Imogen smiled and he reached out and took her hand. 'Listen, how would you like to go off for the day on Saturday? A picnic somewhere. You bring the eats and I'll bring the booze.' Imogen nodded fervently. 'OK,' Nicky said. 'Usual place, ten-thirty tomorrow morning. Wear something casual and we'll go native.'

As she hurried back to the clinic Imogen's heart raced. He *did* care about her! He was going to spend a whole precious day off with her. Somewhere where there was green grass and clear skies and no prying eyes. It would be heaven! She cast up a brief prayer for fair weather but while she waited for Mr Wemyss to return she indulged in a beautiful day-dream of she and Nicky twined together in the little red car while torrential rain beat upon the windows.

She was brought back to earth with a bump by the sight of a wild-eyed Stella in the doorway of the clinic. 'Imo, come quickly! He's gone mad, that kid of yours! Threatening to smash the place up—and he means it!' Imogen's heart sank.

'Do you mean Alexander Dodd?' she said. She was already moving towards the door.

'Is that his name?' Stella said. 'He looks

more like Attila the Hun at the moment. He's in the corridor outside X-ray and the radiologist has sent for the SAS.' Imogen moved as quickly as she could without actually running. The last thing she wanted was to fall foul of the Dragon and running was one of Sister Slater's cardinal sins.

Long before she could see Alexander she could hear him . . . his voice and his stick rattling on walls and radiators as he lashed out at anyone who got in his way. As soon as she rounded the corner she saw how bad the situation was. Alexander was standing with his back to the wall, his face screwed up in anger and terror. He was supporting himself with one stick and using the other as a weapon, brandishing it at anyone who came within range. His mother was begging him to calm down but her words were falling on deaf ears. The radiographer was standing nearby, one hand up to her cheek in dismay.

'What on earth's the matter with him?' she said as Imogen drew near. Imogen looked at her.

'Did anyone say anything to upset him?' she asked. The radiographer shook her head.

'No. I was as nice as I could be with him. I'd done his films and we were waiting until darkroom said they were OK and he could go, and then he suddenly went off the deep end!' Imogen looked at the distraught child.

'What were you saying to him while you

waited?' she insisted and then it came out. 'Nothing. Not a thing that could have upset him. I simply said I'd see him when he came down from the ward . . .' Imogen looked at her in disgust.

'What do you mean, "down from the ward"?' The girl looked at her sheepishly.

'Well, it's obvious he'll have to be re-admitted. Everyone knows that.' Imogen bit her lip. Everyone might know, but it was not everyone's place to discuss it with the child. That should have been left to the surgeon, who would have handled it tactfully. However, there was no point in recriminations. The important thing was to calm the child down.

Before she could begin the peace-making process there was a sudden intervention. Dr Graham, attracted by the noise, was bearing down on them and from the set of her jaw she was none too pleased.

'Who on earth is making all this noise?' she said, fixing Alexander with a baleful eye. His answer was to lunge at her with his stick and she had to step smartly out of range. 'Stop that at once,' she said sternly, glaring at Alexander as though to mesmerise him. Imogen was sure this was the wrong way to deal with him but it was not her place to intervene. Left to herself she would have tried to appease him but she knew what Dr Graham would think of this so she stayed silent.

'Did you hear what I said? I said stop it

at once! Don't be such a baby! A great big boy like you, you should be ashamed of yourself.' Alexander's answer was a roar of defiance.

By now a crowd had gathered—patients, porters, nurses and X-ray staff, all anxious to see Alexander get his come-uppance. Imogen's pity for the little boy was increasing with every minute. It wasn't fair that he should have so many adults ranged against him. Dr Graham on her own was formidable enough!

The next moment Mr Wemyss had pushed his way through the crowd. 'What on earth is going on?' he said, glaring not at Alexander but at the flushed face of the gynaecological registrar. Dr Graham looked back at him, trying to compose her face and make light of the matter.

'We seem to have a slight problem here,' she said sweetly. 'Is he one of yours?' Mr Wemyss glared back at her.

'Yes, he's one of mine. But your method of treatment is wrong, I'm afraid.' Whether or not his words were meant as a rebuke, they went home. Dr Graham bit her beautiful lip and turned away as Mr Wemyss moved towards the little boy.

'Get off! Get off! I've warned you!' The stick flailed wildly and Mr Wemyss stayed where he was. Suddenly he caught sight of Imogen.

'Can you do anything, Nurse Brent?' he asked quietly and Imogen nodded.

'I think so,' she said. 'If you can get everyone to go away.'

As if by magic the crowd melted until Imogen was left alone with the child and the surgeon. She took a deep breath and moved steadily towards Alexander, holding out her arms.

'Come on,' she said. 'You need a drink of orange and a biscuit after all that fuss.' The stick was raised but it wavered and she saw her chance. The next moment she had clasped the child in her arms and lifted him off his feet. He gave a snorting sob and turned his face into her neck, all fight gone out of him.

'Let me take him,' Mr Wemyss said quietly, and Alexander allowed himself to be handed over without protest. As they moved away towards the clinic Imogen saw Dr Graham standing in a doorway, half hidden from view. There was a look of cold, calculated hatred on her face which might have been for Alexander. However, Imogen was fairly sure it was not!

They laid Alexander on a couch and Imogen brought him the promised drink. 'There now,' she said, smoothing his hair from his brow. It was damp with sweat and tears and she fetched cool water in a kidney dish to bathe his face. Mr Wemyss stood silently by until she'd finished and tucked a blanket around the now shivering child. At last he came over.

'Better?' he said to Alexander and received a grudging nod. 'OK. Now we'll talk. What

made you so upset?' The child didn't answer
and Mr Wemyss turned to Imogen. He knew
from bitter experience that Alexander's
mother was less than helpful. 'Do you know
what went wrong, Nurse?' Imogen nodded.

'I think so. Someone in X-ray mentioned his
admission. Well, you know how he feels about
that. He reacted rather violently and things
went from bad to worse.' The surgeon
grimaced.

'Yes. I noticed he was being treated with less
than tact. Who was the fool who upset him in
the first place? No, I know, you won't tell me.
Never mind. The important thing is that
Alexander was upset.'

He sat on the edge of the couch and grasped
the child's small, balled fist. 'Decisions about
your treatment are made by you and I, Alexander, no one else. Except your parents, of
course. If and when you need to come in I'll tell
you. Don't listen to anyone else. Will you
promise me that?' Alexander nodded but there
was still a wary look in his eye.

'Am I coming in?' he asked. Imogen saw a
look of anguish cross the surgeon's face.
Obviously the child needed admission and he
didn't know how to break the news. She took
her courage in both hands and moved forward,
bending until she and Alexander locked eyes.

'Tell me why you hate to come into hospital?' she said. 'I know it's not as nice as home
but it shouldn't be as bad as all that. Perhaps

there's something we can do to make it better for you—but if you don't tell us why you hate it we can't try, can we?'

She held her breath, fearful of what Mr Wemyss's reaction would be, but to her amazement she felt his hand on her shoulder, giving a firm pat of approval. She went on.

'If you tell me what's wrong I promise we'll try and put it right.' There was a long pause and she had almost given up hope when Alexander began to speak.

'It's rotten up there. They treat you like a baby. You don't get no proper food. No tomato sauce. They switch the telly off before the good things come on. I never got to see "The Sweeney" *once* the last time I was in.' Imogen felt her lips twitch. To think half the hospital had been held at bay over a bottle of sauce and the Flying Squad. She composed her face and looked gravely at the child.

'I don't know if I can do anything about the TV. There have to be rules, you know. But I promise I'll bring you some tomato sauce.' Alexander was mollified but reluctant to show it.

'Bet you don't,' he said.

'I will,' Imogen said firmly. The next moment Mr Wemyss moved forward.

'She will come and see you, Alexander. I'll make sure she does. Apart from that, you'll only need to be in a few days. I want to give you a whiff to put you to sleep so I can have a look at those knees of yours. I can look at them properly when you're sound asleep, you know. And then you can go back home, where your mother will serve you gallons of sauce while you watch every television show you want.'

It was not until they were both outside the cubicle that they could collapse into laughter. 'The little devil,' Mr Wemyss said admiringly, and Imogen wiped tears of mirth from her eyes. 'All the same, I think there was more to it than that. I think he feels unsafe in the ward for some reason and it's the thought of you coming to see him that made the difference, whether or not you come bearing tomato sauce.' Imogen had a shrewd idea he was right and she nodded her head.

'Are you going to take him in today? I can pop in to see him tomorrow, there's no problem there.' Mr Wemyss pondered.

'Yes, better strike while the iron's hot. We'll have him in now and I'll do the examination under anaesthesia on Monday afternoon.' So it was arranged, and Alexander went off to the Childrens' Ward while they settled down to the rest of the clinic.

Imogen had felt no particular stress when the scene with Alexander had taken place. She had been too full of sympathy for the child. Now , however, reaction was setting in. As she ushered the last patient out her legs felt like lead. She turned back to begin clearing up and saw Mr Wemyss regarding her with a kindly eye for once.

'Tired?' he asked sympathetically. 'You've had a heavy morning. Heavier than usual. Going three rounds with our friend Alexander is no mean feat!' Imogen smiled.

'I hope he's going to be all right. He's rather a nice little boy really. Not half as fierce as he'd like us to believe. I think he's terrified out of his wits most of the time. His mother feeds his fears and builds up a picture of this place as a kind of torture chamber. She doesn't do it deliberately, I think she's just that kind of woman and her poor little boy has to pay for it.'

Mr Wemyss nodded. 'You should study psychiatry, Nurse Brent. Or perhaps you don't need to. Now I'm going up to communicate your feelings, which I share, to Ward Sister. I want her to ensure that Alexander has every help to settle down up there. In fact, I mean to make sure that he does!' There was a stern note in his voice and Imogen quailed. If he as much as mentioned to the Childrens' Ward sister that she, a lowly probationer, had been airing her views she would be in deep trouble!

Her fear must have shown in her face for Mr Wemyss gave her a conspiratorial smile. 'Don't worry. I shan't mention anything about you. I know the protocol that exists here. You're not supposed to have a thought in your head until you've got your State Registration and then, overnight, you're supposed to become a genius. The logic of that idea has always escaped me but no doubt they have their reasons. And now I must let you get away to lunch. You look tired. Thank you very much for your help this morning, Nurse Brent. See you on Monday.' He moved past her and had nearly reached the door when he turned. 'Will you be going to see Alexander in the morning?' Imogen nodded. 'Good,' he said and went through the doors.

CHAPTER SEVEN

USUALLY Imogen enjoyed a long lie in on her Saturday off but today she was up with the lark. She dispensed with breakfast and made do with a cup of coffee in her room. She knew there was no chance of a bath at that time, with nurses getting ready for duty, so she settled for cleaning her teeth and pulling on jeans and a sweater before she went out to do her shopping.

She bought French bread, butter, home-cooked ham and pâté and crisp salad vegetables. She topped off her purchases with cheese and apples and a large bottle of tomato sauce and hurried back to the home to get ready.

She found the bathroom empty and stepped into the shower with a gasp of pleasure. It was going to be a marvellous day. The hands of the clock showed five minutes to ten when she finally quit her room and ran down the stairs, a bulky holdall in her hand. First of all she had to keep her promise to Alexander Dodd. She crossed the courtyard and made for the ward by the outside stairs. Junior nurses were not encouraged to wander the corridors in their outside clothes. Some people said Matron preferred to believe they didn't have a private life. If they were not in uniform and on duty they didn't exist! As far as Imogen knew there was no rule against visiting the wards but it was best to do it discreetly.

She took out the tomato sauce and left the holdall in the corridor before she went through the ward doors. There were no nursing staff about and she walked quietly up to the door of sister's office. 'Come,' said the authoritative voice of Sister McFarlane when she knocked and Imogen pushed open the door.

'Excuse me, Sister. I wonder if it would be possible for me to see Alexander Dodd. He was admitted from Orthopaedic Outpatients' yesterday and I promised him I'd come and see him.' The elderly sister regarded her solemnly.

'Well, well, another visitor for Mr Dodd. I must ask him to tell me the secret of his charm. He looked to me like a very ordinary little boy but I must have missed something. If he can attract a string of VIP visitors there must be something special about him! Very well, run along Nurse. And don't outstay your welcome!' Imogen knew what that meant. She had five minutes to spend with Alexander and no more. She smiled her thanks and withdrew.

As she entered the ward she half-expected to hear Alexander's defiant voice but there was nothing but the sound of happy children and the burble of the Saturday morning childrens' programme on the TV set at the bottom of the ward. She moved from bed to bed, recognising some of the children, seeing others still in bed or playing with their toys. There was a play pen in the middle of the ward with three beautiful toddlers inside it. She longed to pick them up and cradle them but she wouldn't have dared. She had permission to visit one of Sister McFarlane's patients but that didn't give her *carte blanche*.

She was almost at the bottom of the ward when she saw Alexander's tousled head. He was sitting up, the bed table pulled up to his chest. He was intent on what he was doing, marshalling an army of small soldiers. She was right beside the bed before he noticed her but when he did his face lit up.

'Good job you came. I thought you weren't coming and I was going to make a fuss about it.' She leaned towards him and put her hand on his head. The fair hair had the faint bristle that showed he was no longer a baby and she looked him squarely in the eye when she spoke.

'I said I'd come and see you, Alexander Dodd. You should know better than to think I wouldn't keep my word. Here's your precious tomato sauce and don't get it on the bedclothes or you'll get me shot. Now tell me which war you're fighting and don't let me hear any more nonsense from you.' He grinned and looked down at the assembled army.

'He gave me this lot. He says I'm too big for the toys they have on this ward. He came in before you did and he never said he would.'

Imogen was curious. 'Who came in?' she said. He looked at her impatiently.

'Him, of course. The doctor. Him that was with you yesterday.' Imogen picked up one of the soldiers.

'Do you mean Mr Wemyss?' she asked as nonchalantly as she could. Alexander nodded impatiently.

'Yes. Only it's Dr Wemyss.' Imogen decided against explaining the mysteries of why Fellows of the Royal College of Surgeons were called 'mister' rather than 'doctor' to an eight year-old, even one as bright as Alexander. She was marvelling at the intricacy of the tiny figures in their scarlet uniforms. They must have cost the earth! And he must have been out very early indeed to buy them and deliver them to the ward before ten in the morning. He was a strange man and no mistake!

Long after she had bid Alexander a cheerful farewell and promised to visit him again she was puzzling over the enigmatic man who ruled the Orthopaedic Department. He was double-sided like a coin. Charming one side, chilly the other!

And then she was out in the courtyard once more, the gates lay ahead and the prospect of a whole day with Nicky. If it had not been for the heavy holdall she would have broken into a run. As it was, all thoughts of Alexander and Mr Wemyss fled from her mind. It seemed strange to be slipping out of the bustling hospital. Usually it was quiet and deserted when she went to meet Nicky but today there was activity everywhere. She had to stand aside in the courtyard to allow an urgent stretcher case to be carried into Reception and the porter on the lodge was too busy to acknowledge her as she made her exit.

She'd only walked a few yards when Nicky's car zoomed past her. She turned to the kerb, expecting it to slow and then reverse back to her, but to her amazement it carried on down the road to its usual stopping place. The bag, with its load of food and utensils, was heavy and bumped against her legs as she hurried towards it. At first she thought Nicky hadn't seen her but when she was almost level with the car he climbed out and came round to open the passenger door.

'Let me take that,' he said, reaching for the bag. For a moment she contemplated asking him why he had driven past her but she decided against it. In her heart of hearts she already knew the reason. She had been too near the hospital when he came abreast of her and he wouldn't risk being seen. As they drove away she was wrestling with herself, trying to remember that the life of a young doctor was difficult enough without extra complications but uncomfortably aware that if he really loved her he would have stopped and damn the consequences.

As if he was aware of her discomfort, Nicky began to charm her. 'I'm really looking forward to today, Imo darling. It's so lovely to be driving away from that place . . . right away, where no one can badger me or ask me to sign things or check things or give permission. Today I'm not the ENT houseman, I'm a hobo, a vagabond. You and I, my love, are going to wander the countryside like gypsies. Are you prepared for that?' He glanced sideways at her and smiled and she couldn't help but respond. She nodded but couldn't stop herself from thinking that it all sounded a bit silly.

'Yes, I'm going to be the complete peasant and walk barefoot in the grass', she humoured. Nicky laughed and glanced at her again.

'How abandoned of you! You'd better be careful, darling, or I might get carried away. I've often thought I might be a foot fetishist.' He saw her puzzled expression. 'That's someone who has a thing about feet,' he explained. Suddenly he chuckled. 'And later, I've got a little surprise for you, something up the proverbial sleeve—but don't ask what, because I won't tell you.'

Imogen began to look around her. They were leaving the town behind and moving into green countryside. There was still the odd detached house here and there but soon these too were left behind.

'Where are we going?' she asked. Nicky kept his eyes on the road as he answered.

'We're going up into the hills. I know a marvellous picnic spot with a view over the whole county. There's a wooded glade and a babbling brook and not a habitation for miles. How does that sound?' Imogen almost purred.

'Wonderful. But I warn you now, I probably shan't want to come home.' Nicky was entering into the spirit of the game.

'Then you shan't, little Imo. I'll build you a cabin of twigs just like the pioneers, and we'll lie down at night under a canopy of stars.' It was a delicious thought and Imogen could feel herself unwinding. It was true what Nicky said about needing to get away from the hospital. Now that they were leaving it behind she was shedding all her doubts and uncertainties. He was here, he loved her, they were going to have a glorious day and nothing that Stella or anyone else might say could spoil it.

The place he had chosen for their picnic was as idyllic as he had promised. Acres of lush, green grass, a sparkling stream and only the occasional wandering sheep to disturb them. Nicky produced a rug and the promised bottle of wine and then, to Imogen's delight, he produced a portable cassette player.

'And I've got all your favourite tapes,' he said grandly. '"Romeo and Juliet" and "Scherazade" and a lot of Rachmaninoff. A bit too highbrow for my tastes but I know you love that sort of thing so I borrowed them.' Impulsively Imogen leaned across and kissed his cheek. So he did love her after all!

They went for a walk before lunch, moving hand in hand on the open hillside, and then returned to the car to eat. Nicky had laid the wine in the grass and covered it from the sun and now, when it was opened, it was cool and delicious. He enthused over her choice of food and ate ravenously but when the meal was over there was still a lot to pack away. While they ate they talked, the romantic sound of Rachmaninoff in the background. Somehow the conversation came round to Dr Graham and Mr Wemyss.

'I think he's taken her to the pictures once or twice. I expect she wears him down remorselessly. He probably thinks the cinema is safer and less intimate than a meal or having her round to his place. He never accepts invitations to her flat, I do know that. But he likes entertaining at his place, as long as it's safe.' The idea of old Wemyss having a 'place' was strange to Imogen.

'Where does he live?' she asked. Nicky's mouth rounded.

'Oh, in some style, I can tell you. His people have money. He's got a great big Gothic house on the outskirts of town. Acres of ground and a couple to run it for him. Must cost the earth but he can afford it. Apparently it was a ruin when he bought it and he's restored it to its original state. Does a lot of work himself, so they say.'

Imogen could imagine those huge and capable hands working lovingly on wood and stone, just as they must have picked out toy soldiers for a small and bewildered boy.

'Penny for them,' Nicky said, leaning towards her on the grass. She shook her head, smiling.

'My mind is a complete blank,' she said and lay back to get the full effect of the sun.

For the next half hour they dozed in the sunshine. Nicky's hand crept out across the grass and found hers and they lay there, hands linked, in perfect peace. Eventually Imogen sat up and looked at her watch. It was four o'clock and she could hardly believe it. Nicky sat up too and stretched and when he reached for her she did not pull away. They sank into the cool, green grass and he began to kiss her, starting at her ear, traversing her eyelids and nose, ending at her mouth. When he drew his lips away they lingered on her face and then began to move down over the firm throat.

It felt delicious and half of her wanted it to go on forever. But the other half of her was afraid. The water was getting deeper all the time and she was seized with a desperate longing to feel the ground once more beneath her feet.

'Please, Nicky. Please.' He hesitated for a moment and then he rolled swiftly onto his back.

'Alright, Imo. Don't panic!' There was silence for a moment and then he looked at his watch. 'It's time to go back, anyway. But next

time let's get away for a whole weekend. I
think you'd be a different person if I got you
away from the Lanchester Royal and all it
stands for.' He looked at her, a strange almost
calculating look. 'You are going to come,
aren't you, Imo? I've told you how much I need
a break.' Imogen nodded. She had already
made up her mind that the next time he asked
her she would go. Her nod seemed to please
him and when he spoke again his voice was
cheerful.

'Anyway, now comes my surprise, Imo darling. The perfect end to a perfect day. We're
going back to the flat and I'm going to wait on
you hand and foot.' The next moment he was
pulling her to her feet and they were gathering
up their things.

When they reached the main road Nicky
began to whistle. 'Happy?' he said, looking
sideways at Imogen. She smiled agreement and
they didn't speak again until they were back in
town and driving down a tree-lined avenue.

'Here we are,' Nicky said, snapping on
the handbrake with a flourish. 'La Maison
Fleming!' He leaped out and came round to
open her door, helping her out and guiding her
up the path.

The flat was surprisingly spacious, furnished
with old-fashioned but comfortable chairs and
a low coffee table. Nicky installed her on the
huge sofa and insisted on lifting up her feet and
putting a cushion at her back.

'There now,' he said. 'You sit there while I go and see what's going on in the kitchen.' The next moment he was back with a bottle of wine. He poured and handed it to Imogen. They clinked glasses and sipped.

'Wonderful,' Imogen said and Nicky agreed.

'Right,' he said after a moment, putting down his glass. 'I've got to get back to the kitchen. You stay here and relax.' When he had gone she glanced round the room. There was a bookcase in the corner crowded with medical textbooks and one or two paperback novels. Imogen's lips curved as she noticed the healthy film of dust that covered the textbooks. Obviously they didn't work too hard! Next to the bookcase there was a hi-fi and a stack of records. Imogen was about to cross over and look at them when Nicky reappeared.

'Great minds think alike,' he said. 'What would you like? Beethoven, Beatles or Bacharach?' She settled for Beatles music and lay back as the strains wafted over her.

Some appetizing smells were coming from the kitchen and from time to time she could hear Nicky singing along with the music. She tried to remember when she had last felt so happy. In the end she gave up because she had never felt happy in quite this way before. This was happiness spiced with excitement and uncertainty. 'You're living dangerously, Imogen Brent,' she told herself and shivered a little at the thought of it.

Nicky came back into the room and flicked a red and white checked cloth expertly over the table. 'You do that with great skill,' Imogen said. He tapped the side of his nose with a forefinger.

'You haven't seen half of my many talents yet, cherie.' A moment later he was back with cutlery and napkins and, the finishing touch, a single rose propped in a bottle. 'Wanted to get candles but Jimmy said the insurance wouldn't stand it.' Imogen smiled.

'It looks perfect just as it is' she said.

'Wait till you taste the Chicken Marengo,' was his reply. She raised her brows.

'You mean you can cook Chicken Marengo?' she said. He laughed.

'No. But I can buy it at the freezer centre and heat it up. I'm very good at playing the host.' He went back to the kitchen and Imogen sat there wondering. He certainly was good at playing host, so good he must have had lots of practice.

When he came back into the room, bearing the food, she did her best to make conversation. 'Mr Wemyss did something rather nice this morning . . .' Nicky held up a warning hand.

'I didn't invite you here to give me a diatribe about the virtues of my superiors. So no shop talk! First we eat and then we talk about us. After that, well, we'll see. But now, tuck in and tell me what you think of it.'

The food could have done with a little more warming up but it was good and she told him so. He refilled her glass. 'This is nice,' he said. 'Being here with you, like this. We should have done this ages ago. Would have too, if it hadn't been for old Edgerton hogging the place night after night.'

As if the mention of his name had summoned him up, the door opened and there stood Jimmy Edgerton and behind him a tall blonde staff nurse from the Skin Department.

'Hello folks,' Jimmy said breezily, ushering the girl into the room. 'I see we're just in time for the feast! No, don't argue, Nick! I know I told you we were going to Sharon's place but something came up and we can't, so I'm afraid you'll have to put up with our company for the evening. I'm a little bit old for lurking on park benches.'

With a jerk of his head Nicky summoned Jimmy to follow him into the kitchen. 'Oh dear,' the blonde nurse said. 'There's going to be trouble. I must say Nicky has a nerve, monopolising the flat night after night, making Jimmy stay out of the way. Well, tonight the worm's turned. I'm only sorry it's you, kid. Nicky's friends are usually a bit more . . .' Her words trailed away and Imogen tried to concentrate on her plate and sort out the mixture of emotions that were racing around her brain. The staff nurse tried again.

'I'm Sharon Foster and you're Imogen

Brent, aren't you? You work for the Dragon, heaven help you.' Before Imogen could reply Nicky erupted into the room.

'Have you finished, Imo? Hurry up, that's a good girl. I want to get out of here.' Sharon looked at him, frowning.

'Oh come on, Nick. There's no need to take it like this. Be reasonable. Jimmy's bent over backwards for you up to now. Why do you object to us being here? Are we cramping your famous style?' Nicky's face was thunderous.

'That, if I may say so, is no damn business of yours. Are you ready, Imo?' Imogen gathered up her bag as Jimmy Edgerton appeared from the kitchen.

'You don't have to go, Nick. I've told you that.' He looked at Imogen. 'Don't look so scared, there's a good girl. We have rows like this all the time. I keep telling my friend it's share and share alike but he never seems to get the message.' Before she could reply Nicky had seized her arm and was urging her towards the door. She cast a last despairing look at the others and then followed him down the stairs.

Neither of them spoke on the way back to the hospital. Nicky was still angry and the hard knot of misery in Imogen's chest prevented speech. He drew up at the usual place but he didn't switch off the engine and she knew he was anxious to be rid of her. She reached into the back seat for her holdall. It was heavy, with its load of crockery and uneaten food, and

Nicky had to help her hoist it over the seat. She climbed out, expecting him to get out and carry it at least as far as the gates. But it was not to be. He waited impatiently until she had slung her bag on her shoulder and picked up the holdall, then he muttered a goodbye and closed the door. She stood watching as the car started up and moved away.

Once more the bag bumped against her legs as she hurried towards the hospital gates. It pulled at her shoulder muscles and she paused to swop it from hand to hand. She had just started up again when she heard a voice behind her.

'You seem to be a trifle overburdened, Nurse Brent. Perhaps you should let me have that bag or I'll be called in to treat you for a grievous shoulder lesion. I'm on my way now to deal with a road accident victim—suspected fractures of the thoracic vertebrae—and that's enough for one night. So hand over, there's a good girl.' Mr Wemyss had loomed up along-side her. It was the last straw!

'Thank you very much, but I can manage.' To her horror she sounded tearful and before she could prevent him he had taken the holdall from her.

'What have you got in here? The swag from a burglary?' He was trying to make her laugh but the bag was giving off the rattle of crockery and she was glad that darkness hid her flaming cheeks. Had he seen Nicky letting her out of

the car? And if he had would he realise something was wrong? She had almost to run to
keep up with his strong and athletic stride and,
realising it, he slowed down. The heavy bag
swung from his hand as though it were full of
feathers as he tried once more to divert her.

'Did you get up to see young Dodd?' Imogen
sniffed and tried to answer but the words were
lost in tears.

'Come on,' he said gently. 'It can't be as bad
as all that, surely?' She shook her head fiercely
and blinked away her tears.

'It's nothing. I'm tired, that's all. Yes, I did
see Alexander. He was very taken with his
soldiers. You chose the perfect thing to please
him.'

His voice was low as he replied: 'I wish I
could so easily please other people.' They had
reached the door now and Imogen halted and
held out her hand for the bag. She kept her
head averted for tears were not far away.

'Thank you for helping me, sir. I can manage
now.' He made no move and to her horror she
felt fat tears form in her eyes and begin their
journey down her cheeks. He put down the bag
and moved closer.

'Pull yourself together,' he said softly. 'If
you go in looking like that the jungle drums will
start.' She would have looked up at him but she
felt so ashamed. Suddenly he reached out and
cupped her chin in one huge hand. In his other
hand he held a folded white handkerchief and

he began to wipe her face. His touch was so gentle that she could hardly bear it. She wanted to lean against his comforting bulk and sob out her anguish while the gentle hands went on holding and soothing her. Horrified at her own thoughts she jerked away. This was crazy! He must think her an idiot, and a childish idiot into the bargain.

'Goodnight, sir,' she said, picking up the bag and slipping through the door. As she mounted the stairs she was conscious of him standing stock still in the darkness outside and somehow the thought gave her the courage to face the nurses she passed on the way back to her room.

CHAPTER EIGHT

THE DAY of the dance was a long ordeal for Imogen. She had felt unbelievably flat and miserable since the night at Nicky's flat. She had spent her evenings alone in her room, refusing all Stella's offers of company. Her days had been spent in avoiding Mr Wemyss's sympathetic eyes and dodging Nicky's attempts to catch her in the corridor. Mercifully Stella had generated enough excitement for both of them. Her attitude was mercurial, one moment excited, the next almost weepy. Clive was to rejoin his ship in the early hours of Thursday morning. When the dance was over he must be on his way.

'Will you be coming with Clive and me?' Stella asked casually at break. Too casually! Imogen knew she was fishing. With all her heart she wanted to tell Stella about Nicky but she couldn't bring herself to do it. Eventually she shook her head.

'No thanks, Stella. I wouldn't dream of playing gooseberry. I'll go along with the other girls. We'll see one another there, it's not Wembley Stadium, after all! We'll be on top of one another all night.' But Stella was firm.

'You're coming with us, Imo, and that's

that!' Stella's face was set and Imogen let the matter drop. Suddenly Stella's eyes lit up as she remembered a fascinating titbit.

'Ooh, did I tell you what Maria told me? No, I didn't. Well . . .' She paused to get maximum effect. 'Well, she was in the High Street, just looking in the windows because she hadn't got a cent, when she saw Celia Graham going into "Femme". You know, that boutique opposite the cinema, where the prices are astronomical! Maria says all their clothes come from London. Anyway, after she'd seen Dr Graham go in she went over and looked in the windows. Carefully, so it looked as though she was looking at the display. But she says she saw Celia collecting a dress. Gold lamé or something sparkly. It must have been getting alterations done and she was picking it up. She held it against her and it looked fantastic . . . all for our Roger's benefit, of course!' Imogen looked up, suddenly interested.

'Do you think she will go with Mr Wemyss?' Stella threw back her head and laughed.

'Not if he can help it. All the same, I expect they *will* go together. You know what men are like, they always take the line of least resistance.'

Somehow they got through the afternoon and at quarter to five the Dragon appeared. She ran an eye over the clinic and a speculative finger along the edge of the desk. It came away clean and she gave a nod of satisfaction.

'Good. Well then, as it's the great day I suppose I must let you go early. Make the most of it. It's unlikely to happen again.' Stella's jaw dropped and then she recovered herself.

'Are you going to the dance, Sister?' she said boldly. The Dragon's apron crackled as she turned to Stella.

'I may look in at some time in the evening, Nurse. I trust I will see my staff being circumspect.'

'I know what it means,' Stella said, as they hurried along the corridor. 'It means behaving yourself, doesn't it?' Imogen nodded.

'Something like that,' she said. They were on the upper corridor now, speeding towards the home. Suddenly the doors of the gynae ward opened and a green-clad figure emerged. The hair was hidden by a green cap, a mask drooped below the chin. But the chiselled features of Dr Graham were unmistakable. Even in baggy theatre clothes she looked elegant. At this moment, however, she was preoccupied, walking past them without even a cursory nod.

'It's Gynae Theatre today, isn't it?' Stella said. Imogen nodded. So Dr Graham was having a gruelling afternoon in the heat and tension of the operating theatre. And yet Imogen had no doubt she would arrive at the dance as immaculate as ever. Admittedly she had the advantage of superb looks and figure and the money to do them justice, but there must be iron self-discipline behind that flawless appearance. Imogen thought of her own preparations for the evening, all come to nothing now. The dance would be an ordeal to be endured and somehow the thought of Celia Graham on Mr Wemyss's arm did nothing to help.

Inside her room she took off her shoes and lay down on her bed. The pretty, flower-sprigged dress she'd made hung on the wardrobe but she took no pleasure in it. She wouldn't be short of partners tonight. It was a tradition at the Royal that male staff carried out duty dances. This meant she would be asked to dance by each man she was in contact with during her working day. But what about Nicky? Officially she had no contact with him. Would he ask her to dance? If he did she would say no but if he didn't she would be shamed in front of all the nurses who knew she'd been going out with him. How they must have laughed at her for being a complete and utter fool. She turned over and buried her face in the counterpane. It was a blessed relief to let the tears flow but after a moment she sat up and wiped them away. To be rejected tonight would be bad enough. To stand there red-eyed would be impossible. She tilted her chin to a jaunty angle and went off to tea.

The dining-room was a noisy place at the best of times. Tonight it sounded like a hive of bees. Imogen felt like a leper among the excited faces. She did her best to join in but it wasn't easy. Only the thought of the fuss Stella would make stopped her from deciding not to go to the dance.

Some of the girls had rollers in their hair, others had bathed already and had bright unpainted faces. One of them peered out, dark eyed, from the white mask of a face pack. Imogen looked closer. It was Maria Valent and, sad as she was, Imogen couldn't help a smile as the mask began to tighten and crack and Maria had to run for the bathroom.

'Sometimes I think we're all mad,' Sheila Simpson said, looking round. 'The lengths we go to to catch a man—and they're simply not worth it!' There was a buzz of agreement but Stella shook a resolute head.

'They are,' she said. 'They're worth every agonising minute.'

Stella had already showered and changed so she was able to sit down in front of her mirror and begin her make-up. Imogen stood by and when she was finished she thought Stella had never looked more beautiful. Suddenly Stella's face clouded.

'Look at the time Imo! Here I am being selfish, keeping you here. And you haven't begun to get ready yourself.'

'It won't take me two minutes,' Imogen said grimly. First step was the bathroom. She stepped under the shower and let the water run cold. A few minutes later she was on her way back to her room, refreshed in spite of herself. She sat down at her mirror, intending only the minimum of effort. And then a mood of defiance overtook her. If Cinders was going to the ball she was damn well going to look the part. She applied her make-up with a deft but daring hand, accentuating her huge eyes with violet shadow and applying blusher to the pale cheeks. When she was finished she stood up and slipped the new dress over her head. It was a fine lawn and the main colour was violet. It clung to her small waist and lay in soft folds over her breasts. The puffed sleeves displayed her slim arms and the neckline was low. The final touch was a comb, to which she had fastened tiny artificial violets. They nestled in her dark hair, the perfect foil. She stood up and looked at herself. If she was careful no one would suspect that her heart was breaking!

'We look,' said Stella, halting on the top step, 'simply stunning!' They linked arms and swept down to where Clive was waiting. A few moments later they had reached the swing doors of the Outpatients' waiting room and the music and chatter engulfed them.

Imogen had dreaded that first moment when Clive and Stella must choose between dancing or staying by her side. To her relief Stella turned to her and said, 'I think the hook on my bra has come undone. Shall we go to the cloakroom?' Whether or not it was a subterfuge on Stella's part, Imogen accepted gratefully. They made their excuses to Clive and hurried away.

Even the cloakroom had taken on a festive air. The recreation committee had pinned paper streamers up and someone had put a vase of flowers in a corner. Stella fidgeted with the back of her dress and pronounced herself satisfied and at that moment the door opened and Dr Graham came in. She wore a long, slinky dress of pale gold lamé and her slender neck and fair head rose out of it like a flower. She moved to the washbasin and put down her small gold handbag. She smiled sweetly at the two girls, her eyes raking them. Then she turned to Imogen.

'How sweet you look, like a little milkmaid.' There was no mistaking her meaning and Imogen felt her cheeks flush. 'Did you make your dress? How clever of you.' The tone implied that Imogen had not been clever at all. Imogen looked at Stella and saw storm warnings flashing on the usually cheerful face. If she was going to defuse the situation she would have to be quick!

'Thank you for the compliment, Dr Graham,' she said evenly. 'May I say how lovely your dress is. It must have cost the earth.'

'Good for you, Imo,' Stella said as they made their way back to Clive. The next moment she felt a tap on her shoulder and turned to see a smiling Dr Singh.

'Can this ravishing creature really be the practical Nurse Brent?' he asked playfully. He held out his arms and she moved ahead of him onto the dance floor.

While they danced she tried to respond to his efforts at conversation. 'I'm no dancer,' he said and she perjured herself happily.

'I've known worse,' she laughed, trying to keep her toes out of range. All the same she enjoyed the dance. He was one of her favourite members of staff and when he led her back to her friends she was feeling a little more cheerful. Her eyes flickered around in an attempt to find Nicky. If he was here . . . Even before the thought developed she dismissed it. 'You two go off and dance,' she said. 'I'm alright.' Stella and Clive looked at each other doubtfully and stayed put.

The next moment Imogen's prayers were answered. Rafferty, resplendent in a midnight blue velvet jacket, appeared. 'Can I sit out this dance with you, Nurse Brent? It might be easier on us both.' Clive and Stella moved gratefully away onto the dance floor and Imogen settled down to enjoy Rafferty's patter.

As usual he was intoxicated with his own voice and provided she nodded now and then he was perfectly happy to carry on. Imogen started to look around. Matron was holding court at the head of the room, amid a cluster of senior staff. Imogen picked out Sister Slater, impressive in dark red. A little further over she could see Mr Wemyss, by his side the slender gold figure of Dr Graham. In spite of herself she was looking for Nicky but there was no sign of him.

Suddenly he flashed across her vision, dancing with the glamorous staff nurse from Mens' Surgical. He was wearing a tuxedo that flattered the fair hair and tanned skin. Imogen's hand ached to wave, attract his attention, bring him to her side. Instead she turned to Rafferty. 'What were you saying?' she asked.

A few moments later the music ended and the dancers returned. 'Have you seen the Dragon?' Stella asked, eyes agog. 'She looks magnificent!'

Imogen whirled round as she felt a touch on her shoulder. Mr Wemyss stood there, immaculate in dinner jacket and black bow tie. 'Nurse Brent, I've come to claim you for this dance.' Imogen felt her mouth go suddenly dry. He was formidable enough in the clinic. At close quarters he was terrifying! Nevertheless she allowed herself to be led onto the floor and the next moment a rock-like arm closed around her. They were playing a tango and, somewhat to her surprise, he danced extremely well. Like many big men he was light on his feet and she found she could relax and let him take the lead. They moved together to 'Jealousy' and then the notes of 'Blue Tango' drifted onto the air. Imogen had always loved that tune and she gave herself up to the music.

The firm arm was at her back, the jutting

chin above her ear. She felt herself melting into the music in a way she wouldn't have believed possible. The hand that held hers was gentle and in a funny way it felt right to be here, encircled and safe. As the music ended she felt a tiny surge of regret, but when she looked up into the fierce blue eyes beneath the bristling eyebrows she remembered who he was. 'Thank you very much,' she said formally and only just managed not to add 'sir'.

Suddenly she realised he had not let her go. The music had stopped and people were trickling away from the floor. She moved uneasily inside his arms but he held her tight, forcing her to look up and meet his eyes.

'Why so sad?' he asked. And then again, 'Why?' Imogen looked round desperately. In a moment they would be alone on the floor, the centre of attention.

'Please let me go,' she said and the desperation in her voice did the trick.

He led her back to her place and when the music struck up again he held out his hand to Stella. 'May I steal your lovely partner?' he said to Clive.

'What a thoroughly nice chap,' Clive said as they moved away.

'You should try working with him,' Imogen said drily as she and Clive moved onto the floor. He was an adequate partner but there was none of the magic she had felt in the tango.

When they were back on the edge of the

floor and Mr Wemyss had taken his leave,
Stella gripped her arm. 'Isn't he divine? Where
did he learn to dance like that? He's too good
for Celia Graham. The man's a marvel. You
name it, he does it well!'

Imogen smiled sourly. 'Like taking people
down a peg or two?' she said. 'He does *that*
pretty well.' Stella, too, had suffered from the
surgeon's tongue in the past but she didn't
seem to mind.

'He's not that bad,' she said indulgently.
'And after that dance I'd forgive him anything!' Suddenly her face changed as Nicky
loomed up beside them.

'My dance, I think,' he said confidently and
whisked Imogen on to the floor. 'At last,' he
murmured, holding her close. 'I've been trying
to speak to you all week but you've avoided
me.' Imogen didn't answer. 'You didn't believe that rubbish of Jimmy's—surely not? It
was a bad joke, that's all!' Imogen shook her
head.

'It doesn't matter,' she said, still not looking
at him. 'Let it drop.' He went on cajoling,
explaining everything away as they circled the
floor. In spite of herself she began to believe
him. He sounded so sincere.

'We'll talk about it later,' he said as the
music slowed. As he guided her back towards
Stella she was suddenly aware that Mr
Wemyss's eyes were on her. They were cold
and almost contemptuous, as though she had

committed a *faux pas*. When she turned back, Nicky had vanished.

She watched as he danced first with Miriam Blake, the man-eater, and then with the pretty blonde from Medical Records. She saw Mr Wemyss too, dancing with Dr Graham, and she had to admit they made a perfect couple. Later she saw him guiding a stately Sister Slater around the floor, and whatever he was saying it was making her chuckle.

'There's nothing like a dance for letting you see the other side of people,' Stella said.

Suddenly Mr Wemyss materialised once more at her side. 'Can I presume again, Nurse Brent?' It was a command and Imogen followed him onto the floor, aware of Stella twittering behind. She was also aware of Dr Graham's furious gaze, directed at her across the room but piercing nevertheless. It made her miss a step. 'Never mind,' Mr Wemyss said and held her close until she regained her balance.

Stella could hardly wait for him to take his leave. 'You're the only one he's danced with twice,' she said. 'I know you do his clinic but all the same!' But all Imogen could think of was the sight of Nicky disappearing into the corridor with Miriam Blake.

They went into supper after that. It was a buffet meal and the food was appetising but Imogen wasn't hungry. 'Eat up,' Stella urged. 'We don't get grub like this usually.' Suddenly

Imogen realised Stella and Clive were looking glum.

'Is it time?' she asked and Stella nodded.

'Look after her for me,' Clive said and Imogen nodded.

'I will. But hurry back.' She turned to Stella. 'Off you go. I've had about enough. I'm going to vanish in a moment.' Stella nodded and the next moment she and Clive were making for the door.

A wild idea was forming in Imogen's mind. Nicky had been so convincing on the dance floor, but Sharon Foster had sounded convincing last night. Somehow she had to find the truth. She was just about to leave when she felt a hand on her arm.

'I wonder if I can ask you for another dance, Nurse Brent?' She knew the deep voice belonged to Mr Wemyss and she was ready with her answer.

'I'm terribly sorry, sir. I'm afraid Nurse Roach is waiting for me outside. She's not very well.' His look was enigmatic.

'I see. Then of course I must let you go.' His words were polite, almost formal, and yet they had a whiplash quality that made her feel like a naughty little girl. It was a relief to hurry towards the door and freedom.

Once outside she felt calmer, her thoughts clear. At the moment she only had rumour and assumption about Nicky. She wanted facts. The whole thing hinged on whether or not he had done all the extra duties he had claimed to do. A staff cloakroom loomed up ahead and she stepped inside. In front of the mirror she checked her face. Her eyes looked wide and feverish and she tried to relax. If she was going to nose around the casualty department she mustn't go there looking dishevelled.

She had her story ready and the porter on duty, kindly old Mr Dobson, drank it in without suspicion.

'I've just had a phone call from my mother,' she said, marvelling at the ease with which she could lie when it was necessary. 'She says my aunt had a fall and hurt her arm. They've taken her to hospital but my mother doesn't know which one. I promised her I'd see if it was this one and do what I could.' Mr Dobson clucked with sympathy.

'And you've had to leave the dance—what a shame!' He turned to the big register and ran a finger down. 'What's your auntie's name?'

Imogen swallowed. 'Er . . . Simpson. Mrs Simpson.'

Mr Dobson shook his head. 'No Simpson here. No lady, in fact. Boy of twenty-one, fractured clavicle. Came off a motor bike. Lucky to get off so lightly if you ask me. Girl of sixteen, sprained ankle. No Simpson. Girl with fractured radius, only nineteen. Dr Bates treated them . . . once I got him to answer the phone! He's on duty all night and of course he's in the residence playing cards. They never hang around, these young ones. Not like the old days. Doctors was doctors in those days!' He was off on his favourite subject and Imogen seized her chance.

While he was talking she began to leaf through the register, looking for the last Saturday Nicky had claimed to be on duty. At last she found it and checked the date carefully. It was correct. She ran her finger down the page of cases treated that night. McMichael, Brewis, Tait . . . three would be enough. Surreptitiously she picked up a pencil and scribbled down the numbers of their case notes. Mr Dobson was still droning on and she smiled and nodded to encourage him.

At last she stood up. 'Well, it looks as though I'm on a wild goose chase. She'd have been here by now if it was this hospital.' The porter nodded.

'I'll watch out for her, if you like. Simpson. I'll remember.'

Imogen thanked him and made for the door, the scrap of paper clutched in her hand. As she turned towards the Records Department a tiny ray of hope sprang up in her mind. If Nicky had treated these patients it would mean he was telling the truth and Sharon Foster had lied.

She was so preoccupied that she didn't see the figure advancing towards her along the otherwise deserted corridor. 'Are you all right, Nurse Brent?' She looked up into the concerned face of Mr Wemyss.

'Yes. Yes, I'm perfectly alright thank you.' He reached out and gripped her arm.

'You don't look it. You look dreadful. I knew something was wrong, that's why I followed you.' Imogen felt a sudden anger. How dare he follow her, pry into her affairs?

She pulled her arm free and moved past him. 'I'm perfectly all right. There was something I had to check, that's all. And now I'm going back. Goodnight, sir.' She hurried along the corridor that led to Records, hoping against hope he wouldn't notice she was going in the opposite direction to the nurses' home.

The records office was unlocked and deserted. She let herself in and shut the door quietly behind her. She wasn't sure whether or not it was out of bounds to off-duty nurses but in any event she didn't want anyone to see her. She switched on the light and looked at the paper. The numbers were consecutive and should all be together somewhere in the files that lined the room. She wandered up and down until she found what she was looking for. McMichael, Brewis, Tait. She pulled them out and laid them on the desk. She recognised Jimmy Edgerton's handwriting before she saw his name printed in the space for the doctor in attendance. She checked another. And another. *All* Edgerton. For a moment her mind flirted with the possibility of yet another mistake but the hope was stillborn. Nicky was a liar and a cheat. She closed the case notes and returned them to the files before switching off the light.

It was dark outside and in here, shrouded by the tall files, it was even darker. She leaned against one of the uprights and closed her eyes. Why did life have to be so painful? A tear burned its way to the corner of her eye. 'I can't bear it,' she said in a small voice and covered her face with her hands. Suddenly the light flared.

'Come on, it can't possibly be as bad as that.' She hadn't heard Mr Wemyss come into the room. He must have followed her. She felt her cheeks flame. How dare he! He put a hand into his pocket and drew out a large white handkerchief.

'You're making an awful mess of your face. Wipe it up, there's a good girl, and then tell me what's wrong.' Imogen's feeling oscillated between a desire to slap his face and a longing to melt into those large and capable arms and sob out the whole story. If she wasn't careful she would make an even bigger fool of herself than she had already! She drew herself up and fished in the side pocket of her dress for her own hanky.

'I've got one,' she said, pulling out a small square of cambric.

'Yes, you have,' he said. 'But it's no earthly use, is it? I've told you before, Nurse Brent. A good nurse always uses the proper tools for the job.' She knew he was trying to make her laugh but it only made her feel angry.

'I can manage, thank you!' Suddenly he moved forward and grabbed her arms. The hands she had seen move gently over his patients were hard and she winced at the contact, but he didn't let go. Instead he shook her slightly and when he spoke his voice was full of fury.

'You expect me to go away, don't you? I can see it in your face. You expect me to turn on my heel and go away, leaving you here to break your heart. Well, I can't and I won't! I don't know quite what's going on here but I think I know a little of it. Somehow you've found out about young Fleming and it hurts! It hurts like hell! Well, love *is* painful, Nurse Brent. That much is true.' There was a pause and then he spoke again. 'Have I guessed correctly?' It seemed ridiculous to go on pretending.

'If you let me go and give me the handkerchief I'll tell you,' she relented in a small voice. He released her immediately and gave her the handkerchief. She wiped her eyes and then, almost defiantly, blew her nose.

'I'll let you have this back when it's washed,' she said, and suddenly, amazingly, they were both laughing.

'That's better,' he said in relieved tones. He reached out and took her arm, urging her towards a chair. 'Sit down,' he said and pulled up another chair for himself.

'I've been checking up on Nicky,' she said.

'He keeps telling me he's on duty when he's not. And I'm not his only girl—there are others. I wouldn't believe it when Sharon said it but I've checked. I've looked up the case notes of people he should have treated and now I know it's true.' He looked down at his hands for a moment. When he spoke his voice was gentle.

'Did you care for him very much, Nurse Brent?' She noticed that he used the past tense as though, for him, love would surely die when trust was betrayed. Imogen nodded.

'Yes, I did. I do, I suppose.' For some reason this remark roused him to fury.

'You *do*! How typical! He's treated you abominably and now you're going to lie there, like a discarded dressing, until he deigns to come along with some excuse and pick you up again!' His words were so true that they stung her to a denial.

'I won't! I won't be such a fool again. You can be sure of that!' She stood up suddenly and made for the door but he reached out and clasped her arm.

'Are you sure? Have you really learned your lesson?' She swung round, eyes blazing.

'I'm sorry but I don't see that's any business of yours!' His eyes burned into her and his words gushed out like molten lava.

'You don't? You don't see a lot of things you should see!' It was almost dark now in the deserted office. Dark and silent except for the pool of light in which they stood and the troubled breathing of the man who loomed over her.

Suddenly she was afraid. Tears were still not far away and she couldn't risk making a fool of herself again. And yet when he reached out for her it was so comforting! She went like a lamb, folded against him, feeling her tensions slip away from her like melting snow. Suddenly reason reasserted herself. She wasn't sure what was happening but whatever it was it was getting out of control. Swiftly she tugged herself free and slipped past him.

'I must go, sir. Thank you for being so kind. Goodnight.' The next moment she was through the door and speeding towards safety.

CHAPTER NINE

SOMEWHAT to her amazement Imogen slept soundly through the night, but she woke early. She lay with her eyes shut, unwilling to face the day. There was not just her disillusionment with Nicky, though that would have been enough on its own. There was also the embarrassment of having to face Mr Wemyss. She opened one eye and looked at the crumpled handkerchief lying on her dressing table. So it hadn't been a bad dream, after all.

Remembering the feel of his arms around her on the dance floor, his kindness to her in the records office, his harsh breathing in the few moments before she had made her escape, she was at a loss to understand his behaviour. If she hadn't known better she would have thought he was acting like a man in love. The foolishness of the thought made her wriggle down into the bed and turn her face into the pillow. Such an idea was crazy!

And yet he had touched her so gently when she was sad, reacted so angrily when he thought she was being soft on Nicky. So he must care. In some strange way he minded about her unhappiness. Perhaps it was simply professional concern? If she went to pieces she would be less efficient, run his clinic less smoothly. A grim smile crept round her mouth. Yes, that was it. She was a tool, a piece of equipment, and as such she must be well-maintained, kept in good working order, if she was to serve him to maximum capacity! Even as she thought it she knew it wasn't true. His concern, the way he had left the dance and followed her around the hospital . . . those things betokened something more than the desire for a smooth-running clinic.

She lay for a moment trying hard not to think about anything and then she flung back the covers and jumped out of bed. There was only one thing to do when you were mixed up. Work! 'Please let it be a busy clinic,' she begged out loud. 'So busy that I don't have to look into that arrogant face.' A spasm of conscience shook her as she remembered how Mr Wemyss had looked at her the night before.

'Tell me what's wrong,' he had asked in the kindest way. She stood for a moment, remembering a lot of things about her boss—his gentleness and kind words and toy soldiers bought for a little boy. She had felt bad enough when she woke, now she felt worse.

She still felt miserable when she sat down at the breakfast table but Stella was too taken up with her own misery to notice. 'Cheer up,' Imogen said at last. 'You'll get letters and post cards and you have his home leaves to look forward to.' Stella managed a small smile.

'I suppose you're right,' she agreed and began to eat her breakfast.

To Imogen's relief the waiting-room was full
when they reached the Orthopaedic Department. She had been hoping for a busy day and
it looked as though her wish had been granted.
One of the stretcher cases caught her eye, an
elderly man with a face like a rosy apple. He
had been admitted a few weeks before with a
fractured pelvis. A few weeks of bed rest had
solved his problem but as soon as he had
returned home he had fallen again, this time
over a runaway puppy. This time he had fractured his femur and Imogen had been full of
sympathy for his misfortune. Today, however,
he seemed well and cheerful.

'Mr Fletcher,' she greeted him warmly.
'How are you today? Come to see Mr
Wemyss?' He nodded.

'Indeed I have . . . and what they've got me
on this thing for I don't know! I'm as sharp
on my pins as a four-year old. Wait till I get in
that clinic, I'll show you!' He twinkled up at
Imogen. 'How about you, Nurse? You're a
bonny lass. D'you feel like taking me on?'
Imogen burst into laughter.

'I'll have to turn you down, Mr Fletcher!'
She squeezed his hand and turned away. He
would be all right. With that kind of spirit he
couldn't fail.

The clinic began and reached its usual fever
pitch within minutes. Mr Fletcher came and

went away happily on sticks. 'I told you,' he said as he made his way out, 'I told you he'd have me on me feet in no time.' Mr Wemyss had laughed and joked with the old man but with Imogen he was haughty and withdrawn. It was hard to reconcile this autocratic, demanding figure with the man who had shown her such kindness and sympathy the night before. Today he was not in a sympathetic mood!

'You've given me the wrong notes, Nurse.'

'I said a Histology Request form, not a Path. slip!'

'Can't you do something about that clutter?'

'Hurry, hurry Nurse! Time is at a premium this morning.'

The more she was chivvied, the more mistakes Imogen made. Usually she was efficient and alert. Today she responded sluggishly to his many demands, muddling case notes, dropping instruments, directing him to wrong cubicles and putting the wrong patients at the desk for his attention.

She tried hard to cope, running hither and thither to meet his demands, but it seemed the more she achieved the more he wanted. By break time she was close to weeping and it was a relief to get away for coffee. She made no mention of her troubles to Stella but she could see her friend regarding her with a worried eye.

As soon as she got back to the clinic the cold war resumed. She had put two fractured femora in adjoining cubicles and Mr Wemyss objected. 'It takes too long to get them up and dressed and out again. One would have been quite enough for the time being.' Imogen knew he was right but a small voice of defiance inside her decided to argue the point.

'I'm sorry, sir. I did what I thought was best.' He turned to her and his expression seemed angry beyond all proportion.

'I'm sure you always do what you think is best, Nurse Brent. The trouble is your judgment is so unsound!' Imogen felt hot tears sting her eyes and turned away. It would never do to break down and cry in front of the patients and, apart from that, there was no way she was going to allow this odious man to see her cry, to know that his words had hurt her!

She turned on her heel and walked into an empty cubicle, swishing the curtain behind her. She walked across to the mirror and stood there, staring at her reflection, trying hard to regain her composure. Her face stared back at her, paper-white with huge dark holes for eyes. She put up a hand and settled her cap on her head. In a moment she must go back to her duty and she didn't know if she could manage it. It was crazy but she felt as though Mr Wemyss had betrayed her, turning on her this morning after his tenderness the night before. And yet she had no right to expect anything from him and he had every right to expect her to get on with her job. She took a deep breath and got ready to face the music.

But before she could move the curtains parted and Mr Wemyss stepped inside the cubicle. Imogen went on staring into the mirror as though her life depended on it, watching him move forward until he was close behind her. She dropped her eyes as she felt a gentle hand upon her shoulder.

'I'm sorry. I really am so sorry! I've been a bear this morning, for reasons of my own. You haven't deserved a word of it. Will you forgive me?' The normally booming, authoritative voice was strangely soft and it was too much for Imogen. Tears began to gather in her eyes and roll unhindered down her cheeks. 'Please, oh please, don't cry. I can't bear it!' He grasped her shoulders and turned her to face him.

'Look Nurse Brent . . . oh, this is ridiculous—*Imogen!* There's so much I need to say to you but this is not the place. Help me to finish this clinic and then we'll sort things out.' Imogen was lost for words. It was not so much what he was saying as the way he was saying it that disturbed her. He was talking to her as though they were on the most close and intimate terms and his hands had not left her shoulders. Suddenly she had a vivid picture of the curtains parting once more and the Dragon appearing! The prospect was so terrifying that she was seized with a sudden wild desire to laugh out loud. Here she was, a nurse in training, standing in a deserted cubicle with a senior consultant, who was talking to her in the strangest fashion. It must be a fantasy, a figment of her imagination! Whatever it was she wished the ground would suddenly open and swallow her up. She could see no other way of escape!

As if sent from heaven, a loud noise came from outside the cubicle. Startled, Mr Wemyss relaxed his grip and turned in the direction of the noise. Imogen wrenched herself free and the next moment she had pulled aside the curtain and was out in the clinic.

The sitting patients were looking at her in the most peculiar way and she saw that a pair of crutches stacked against the wall had clattered to the floor. She hurried to retrieve them and as she did so she heard Mr Wemyss come back into the clinic and take his place at the desk. When she straightened up and replaced the crutches her face was resolute and the surgeon, too, appeared anxious to forget what had happened inside the screens. He gave his undivided attention to the patient at the desk, a man with one finger curved down into his palm.

'I can't straighten it, Doctor. No matter how hard I try.' Mr Wemyss nodded.

'I know, it's quite fixed, isn't it? But we can put it right for you. What you have there is known as a Dupuytren's contracture. Quite common and not at all dangerous. I won't go into all the technical details except to say that if we have you in and give you a whiff of anaesthetic we can fix it quite easily.' He talked on for a few moments until the man's anxious face had relaxed and then turned him over to Imogen.

For the rest of the morning the consultant was polite and helpful and they got through the remaining patients without too much trouble. Imogen made sure that she was within sight and sound of Sister Slater when it was time for Mr Wemyss to go and he swept off with his usual courteous, 'Thank you, Nurse.'

Predictably the afternoon dragged. Stella tried hard to be philosophical about the loss of Clive but she was subdued. 'I really think it must be love, Imo. It's a funny feeling. As though your insides have turned to feathers and they're all fluttering up and down inside your chest.' Imogen thought that was a very good description of love. When she had been with Nicky she had felt like that, confused and agitated and not at all her normal self. And now the feathers had turned to lead and were lying heavily about her heart. She sighed and got on with her work.

At Sister Slater's behest they tidied the clinic. They tidied the linen cupboard. They tidied and checked the drug cupboard under the Dragon's eagle eye. 'When there's nothing left to tidy,' Stella said, 'she'll tell us to go back to the beginning again. Like the Forth Bridge. On and on forever and ever.'

Sister Slater appeared at five to five, cast a critical eye over everything and sent them on their way. 'Try and bear up, Nurse Roach,' was her final remark. 'I have a strange feeling you haven't seen the last of that young man.' Stella was too astonished to reply but as they hurried along the corridor she turned to Imogen.

'Did you hear that? I swear I'm going to pray for the Dragon, tonight, Imo! After all the terrible things I've said about her, the times I've plotted how to do away with her and not get caught . . . and then she says something like that! As though she really cared about Clive and me. It makes you ashamed, doesn't it?'

Imogen didn't want to sound smug but she couldn't resist rubbing it in a little. 'I told you she was OK. I *like* working for her. She really cares about the patients. And her staff. Really cares, not just pretends and tries to win popularity. She notices everything and she can turn a blind eye when she thinks it's for the best.' Stella was nodding.

'You're right, Imo. By the time we leave her department we'll be the two best-trained, most disciplined nurses Lanchester Royal ever turned out. Or we'll be ready for the rubber room at the funny farm . . . I'm not sure which!'

Imogen took a mock swipe at Stella but the door of the nurses' home had loomed up and Stella ducked through to safety. They had already decided to spend the evening together and after tea they settled in Imogen's room. To

Imogen's relief Stella was content to babble happily away about Clive and the rosy future she saw ahead. Imogen had been afraid that Stella might probe and ask awkward questions. If she was subjected to the third degree it was quite possible she might break down and tell Stella too much, not only about Nicky but about Roger Wemyss as well. For in spite of herself that tall, forbidding figure was occupying more and more of her thoughts.

After a while the conversation turned to whether or not they should watch television. They were still trying to decide when the phone rang in the corridor outside. 'I'll get it,' Imogen said and made for the door. She picked up the phone.

'Nurses' home. Imogen Brent speaking.' Back came Rafferty's unmistakable voice.

'It's Rafferty here, Nurse Brent. I'm in the porter's lodge. There's two whacking great bouquets of flowers here. One for Nurse Roach and one for you. They wouldn't bring them up because it's their last delivery and they're already over time. Do you know where Nurse Roach is tonight?' Imogen was taken aback but she managed to stammer out a reply.

'She's here with me. Shall we come down?' Rafferty was in his usual obliging mood.

'No, it's OK. I'm coming over your way in a tick. I'll bring them up for you. I hope you're all decent in that harem up there. I'm just a

young bloke and I don't want no shocks.'
Imogen chuckled.

'I'll tell the girls you're on your way up, shall
I? Then they can prepare a proper welcome for
you.' She was laughing as she replaced the
phone but as she made her way back to her
room she was puzzled. Flowers for Stella she
could understand. It was just the sort of thing
Clive would do. But flowers for her? Could
they be from Nicky? Sternly she took herself in
hand. She was being stupid. They would probably be from Clive, his way of saying thank you
to her for looking after Stella while he was
away.

When she reached the door of her room she
composed her face. She wanted the flowers to
be a complete surprise. 'Who was it?' Stella
asked, and Imogen shrugged.

'They wanted to speak to Maria but I told
them she was off duty and had gone home.
They'll ring back.' Stella nodded and got on
with making coffee while Imogen sat with an
ear trained for Rafferty's approach.

He was there within five minutes, whistling
'Red Roses for a Blue Lady'. Imogen sat still
when the knock came and it was Stella who
opened the door. In one arm Rafferty had a
huge bunch of red roses. In his other hand he
had the most beautiful posy Imogen had ever
seen. White stephanotis and freesias in delicate
shades of pink.

'Good Lord!' Stella squealed and then, as

Rafferty held out the roses, the tears came. Tears of laughter and joy and coming from the heart!

'I'll never understand women,' Rafferty grumbled as he held out the posy to Imogen. 'A bloke does nice things to please them and they turn on the tap.'

Imogen could hear Stella weeping with delight but her own eyes were fixed on the magical spray in her hand. There was a small card wired to it and she turned it over. It bore one word . . . 'Sorry'. There was no signature but the handwriting was unmistakable. She had seen it in the clinic this morning, watched the strong hand that made it gliding over the case notes. She looked up to find Stella's eyes fixed on her.

'They're gorgeous, Imo. Who sent them?' Imogen looked up, overcome with embarrassment. She couldn't say. She daren't! The thought of the way Stella's face would light up at the news terrified her.

'Nicky,' she said hastily. 'Nicky sent them.' As she turned away she wondered why she had told a lie. It would only cause more complications later on. But the next moment Stella was fussing over her roses, the posy forgotten. Long after she had gone back to her own room Imogen sat on, looking in rapture at the fragile blossoms and puzzling over the enigmatic man who had sent them.

CHAPTER TEN

ALL THROUGH Friday the fog rolled up, blanketing the hospital in a grey mist. 'I've never known anything like it at this time of the year,' Rafferty said, peering out at the shrouded courtyard. Privately, Imogen thought the weather had come out in sympathy with her and with Stella. In spite of the beautiful flowers Roger Wemyss had sent her she still felt low and Stella was visibly pining for Clive.

Imogen had felt acutely embarrassed as she approached the clinic that morning. Should she say thank you for the flowers as soon as Mr Wemyss arrived? There had been no name on the card so she could play dumb. On the whole she felt she should behave as though nothing had happened and say her thank you later in private when an opportunity arose. She shuddered at the thought of that private moment but she knew it would come.

In the event she had worried in vain. Mr Wemyss greeted her briefly and got straight down to work, leaving no time for private conversation. As if he sensed her inner conflict he was co-operative and easy to deal with during the morning clinic but he seemed reserved, as though he were quite glad to distance himself from her and the intimacy they had enjoyed after the dance and in the clinic yesterday. It suited Imogen. She had no desire to be close to Mr Wemyss or anyone else of the male gender.

Throughout the day, as she went about her work, she caught glimpses of Nicky on the hospital corridors. Once she turned a corner and saw him only yards away. He lifted a hand to attract her attention but she turned resolutely away and went in another direction.

When the morning clinic was over she held the door open for Mr Wemyss to leave. 'Thank you for the flowers,' she said quietly, her eyes fixed on her feet. 'It was very kind but there was no need.' There was silence until she was forced to look up and meet his eyes.

'There was every need,' he said. The next moment he was gone.

'Thank heaven that's over,' Stella said gloomily as they came off duty. 'All I want to do now is get back to my room and weep. I can't even look out of the windows for relief . . . the fog's getting thicker.'

Imogen patted her arm. 'Come on, let's see some positive thinking. Count how many days it will be until he comes back and then work out what you're going to do with them.' Stella's reply was succinct.

'Pine. That's what I'm going to do. Pine!' Imogen tried to laugh it off but she could see that Stella's gloom went very deep.

'Come into my room after tea and we'll have a good old chin-wag,' she suggested. Later on, when Stella had accepted the offer, Imogen wondered if she had done a silly thing. If they were going to chat what would they chat about? Sooner or later, knowing Stella, the conversation would get around to Nicky. Or, to be exact, Nicky's shortcomings. In the past she had defended him. She didn't feel like doing that now, but if she didn't Stella would realise she knew the truth about him. And if they talked about Stella's other favourite topic, Roger Wemyss, it could be even more dangerous. As she ate her tea Imogen was trying to think of safe topics of conversation. If she had known what lay ahead she needn't have bothered!

They had just settled in Imogen's room when they heard the phone ring in the corridor outside. Stella sat bolt upright. 'Could that possibly be Clive?' she asked in a breathless voice. 'Oh could it, could it, Imo?' Imogen shrugged. She had a nasty feeling it might be Nicky ringing up to repair fences. Well, he would be wasting his time. They both held their breath as the ringing stopped and then, before they could exchange a word, there was a thunderous rapping on the door and they heard Sheila Simpson's voice.

'Out! Everybody out! It's disaster drill. Get a move on everybody. This time it's for real!'

Imogen's startled eyes met Stella's equally startled ones. Disaster drill? They had gone through the details again and again with Sister Tutor, what they must all do if a real emergency struck Lanchester, but somehow it had seemed unlikely that it would ever happen. They both leaped to their feet.

'What can it be?' Stella said, struggling back into her shoes. Imogen was reaching for her discarded cap and apron.

'I don't know, but we'd better find out,' she said. Like most other hospitals Lanchester Royal had a well defined arrangement for dealing with major emergencies. New nurses were told about it in their first few weeks of training. Senior staff knew it by heart and it involved every single person in the hospital. In time of national or local emergency every member of staff was to report for duty in the main Casualty waiting room. There they would be detailed off by whoever was in charge of Casualty and sent to wherever they might be needed, not necessarily the place where they worked normally.

They had practised it in theory so often but now, as off-duty nurses tumbled down the stairs towards the main body of the hospital, Imogen reflected that theory was very different from the real thing. Everyone looked surprised, even slightly scared. She had butterflies in her own tummy that seemed to have six foot wing spans. 'Whatever can it be?' Stella said as they hurried along the corridor. 'I mean, we haven't heard any bangs or anything like that. And it's a bit too sudden for plague.' In spite of her anxiety Imogen laughed.

'You are an idiot, Stella. Plague indeed!'

The next moment they reached the crowded casualty department and reported to the senior sister who was standing at the reception desk. 'Brent, Roach,' she said, ticking them off. 'Roach to the dressing clinic, Brent, you'd better . . .' She never finished her sentence.

'Nurse Brent will be assisting me,' Mr Wemyss said, moving swiftly past them. Imogen looked at casualty sister, who hesitated and then gave a startled nod. Imogen followed the tall, white-coated figure as he moved towards casualty reception. She was dying to know exactly what was going on. On her way down she had heard all sorts of rumours. A gas tank had exploded, there had been a huge warehouse fire . . . teenagers were rioting in the town centre! One girl had even suggested that war had broken out! Obviously none of these things were true. Casualty sister had been too self-possessed for that. But something was going on, something of major proportions.

The outer doors burst open to admit a trolley and behind it another and another. Just then, out of the corner of her eye, she saw Rafferty. Rafferty was sure to know. She took a look at Mr Wemyss. He was still striding ahead of her, as though ignorant of her presence. She de-

cided to take a risk and ask Rafferty what was
going on.

'It's the fog, isn't it!' he said. 'That and those
idiots on four wheels out there. The Police
Sergeant said they're piling into one another
like a pack of lemmings.' So that was it! A
multiple pile-up on the motorway. That meant
casualties—multiple injuries, head injuries,
facial lacerations and stove-in chests. She took
a deep breath and mentally girded her loins for
the coming fray. She reached Mr Wemyss as he
turned to look for her.

'Ah! You're there, Nurse Brent. Good.
Let's get cracking!' The next moment the
onslaught was upon them. It was strange to see
the lordly orthopaedic surgeon acting as a re-
ceiving officer, but when disaster drill was in
operation protocol went out of the window.
Everyone did whatever job came to hand. The
casualties were mostly in a state of shock and
Mr Wemyss and Imogen began to check them
over, make a rough list of their injuries on a
case sheet and pass them on for further treatment. Imogen watched his hands moving
swiftly but gently over the patient's limbs and
marvelled at their expertise. He probed gently
at thorax and abdomen and felt along the
limbs. Where there was a suspicion of a head
injury he tested for reflexes, all the time mur-
muring reassurances as he shone the probing
beam into their eyes. Once or twice one of
the victims clutched at him, weeping with pain

and fear, and again Imogen was struck with his gentleness as he disentangled himself. He never failed to promise them all would be well.

Speed was vital and he moved along the line of stretchers without delay, but every patient was relieved by his presence. Imogen did what she could to clean and comfort the patients as he examined them and by now they'd been joined by a medical records clerk, who noted down Mr Wemyss's comments. At one stage she looked up and caught Imogen's eye. 'We've practised this routine for years and it looks as though it's paid off!' she grinned confidently.

Most of the accident victims were suffering from facial lacerations. Once Mr Wemyss made sure they had no other severe injuries they were wheeled away to have their wounds cleaned and sutured. Later on they would need the attention of a plastic surgeon, but that would have to wait until the bruising and swelling had disappeared.

'Lucky you were wearing a seat belt, old chap,' Mr Wemyss told one patient who had escaped with comparatively minor injuries.

The next patient had not been so lucky, thrown forward against the dashboard. She had comminuted fractures of her left radius and ulna, a compound fracture of her humerus on the same side, facial lacerations and nasal fractures. As Imogen tried to clean the debris from her wounds Mr Wemyss satisfied himself there was no brain or allied damage.

'It could have been a lot worse,' he said to the girl consolingly. She was weeping uncontrollably, tears mingling with the dirt on her blood-stained face.

The worst cases were the crush injuries of the chest and as he gave them rapt attention Imogen remembered that Roger Wemyss had written a famous pamphlet on chest injuries. Sister Tutor had referred to it in tones of awe.

'I don't know whether or not you realise it, nurses, but we are very lucky to have Mr Wemyss at Lanchester Royal. He's one of the country's leading orthopaedic specialists with a growing reputation. And he's still quite a young man!'

Looking at him now, cuffs turned back from the strong wrists, fair hair falling across his forehead, giving his whole attention to his patient, Imogen realised he *was* young to be a consultant. In the more formal atmosphere of the clinic he was sometimes a forbidding and distant figure. Here, where there was neither time nor room for formality, she was seeing his true self. He looked up and caught her eye. 'This takes me back, Nurse Brent. Back to the far-off days when I was a junior houseman here at the Royal and you were no doubt making daisy chains in your back garden.'

Before Imogen could think of a suitable reply they were interrupted by the sight of Dr

Graham approaching them, clad in the shape-
less green garments of the theatre. 'Roger,' she
said, ignoring Imogen, 'Roger, I've got this
woman in Theatre and I think she's got fractured pubic rami. The abdomen is distended
and there's some guarding. Could you have a
look at her?' She glanced up at him from under
long lashes. Even at a moment of stress she was
obviously very much aware of him as a man.
He nodded gravely.

'Of course, Celia. I'll be along in a moment.'
She stood still, determined to carry him off
with her. She gave a little laugh.

'I've devoted myself so much to my own
subject that I've grown rusty on my orthopaedics and my general surgery. You'll have to
give me some lessons when all this is over. Help
me to brush up my technique.' There was a
cocquettish note in her voice and Imogen saw a
small frown darken Mr Wemyss's brow. Here,
surrounded by injured people, he was in no
mood to play flirtatious games.

'If you want to polish your general surgery,
Celia, you should ask Forsyth! It's not
my province except in these abnormal circum-
stances.' Suddenly Imogen was aware of Celia
Graham's eyes upon her. The older woman's
brows arched in a preremptory way. There
was no mistaking its meaning. 'Go away,' her
eyes flashed. Imogen turned, but before Dr
Graham could capitalise on her going Mr
Wemyss spoke up.

'I said I'll come in a moment, Celia. You run along. I'm sure they need you back there. I'll be along as soon as I can.' There was nothing Dr Graham could do but turn on her heel and stalk off but Imogen could see fury in every line of the retreating figure.

A few moments later Mr Wemyss straightened up and looked around. 'Do you think I can nip off to Theatre now, Nurse Brent? I'd better have a look at that lady in case she has some internal injury.' Imogen was removing tiny pieces of glass from a jagged cut on a patient's forehead.

'Yes sir. I'll finish this and have it ready for you when you come back.' His tone had implied that he didn't think the matter of Dr Graham's patient too serious and Imogen had the feeling he would have liked to say more. She was glad he hadn't, she would have found it an embarrassment. He was away for only a few minutes and when he came back he looked relieved.

'It was a false alarm. She's got a fractured pubic ramus all right, but there's no visceral involvement. I didn't think there would be.'

It seemed as though the stream of casualties was never-ending. The air was loud with moaning and the agitated enquiries of patients asking about their fellow victims. There were policemen everywhere, trying to make order out of chaos, but the hero of the evening was Rafferty. He was here, there and everywhere.

Finding necessary equipment, locating case notes, matching up friends and relatives who had been separated in the mêlée and giving everyone a cheery word. Imogen saw him bending over an old lady on a trolley, holding her hand and promising her a nice cup of tea before too long. She clung to him as though he were her long lost son until he gave her hand a pat, tucked it inside the blanket and moved on. Several times he helped Mr Wemyss lift a patient so that an examination could proceed, and the two men seemed to work together in perfect harmony. It mattered little that one was a senior consultant and the other an ancillary worker. The hospital was under fire and they were nothing else but colleagues.

Only once did she see Mr Wemyss exhibit signs of stress and then he simply raised his arms and flexed his shoulders once or twice. The next moment he gave his whole attention to the small boy who lay quietly on the stretcher, waiting his turn. As always he was wonderful with children.

'Well, you *have* been in the wars. You're quite the wounded soldier, aren't you? Do you remember much about it?' Imogen knew he was not asking an idle question. Getting the child to respond was an important part of the examination and eventual diagnosis. The child shook his head. 'Can't you tell me anything about it?' Mr Wemyss asked gently.

'There was a bump,' the child said, trying to

be helpful. 'There was a bump and then a kind of cracking noise and then my mum was shouting.' Suddenly he remembered his mother and started to look desperately around.

'OK, OK,' Mr Wemyss said soothingly. 'What's your name? Nurse Brent here will find your mum for you.' The child bit his lip.

'Michael Baker. My mum's Mrs Baker.' Mr Wemyss patted his hand.

'All right, Michael Baker. We'll find her for you right away. Will you lie here and get some rest while we do it?' The child nodded, gazing up trustingly, and Mr Wemyss turned to Imogen. 'Is there any chance of locating his mother? Rafferty might be able to help you.' Imogen nodded.

'Leave it to me, sir. If you can spare me I'll go right away.' He was deftly covering up the child as he nodded.

'Yes. Cut along. Miss Bates will help me till you get back. But hurry.' Imogen threw a grateful glance at the records clerk and sped away.

She found Rafferty in the doorway, sneaking a puff on a cigarette. He half choked when she came up behind him. 'Good Lord! You didn't half give me a turn. I thought it was casualty sister sneaking up on me.' Imogen smiled.

'I don't think she'd blame you for having a crafty smoke on a night like this, not now that things are dying down. You've been working like a slave, everyone says so. Anyway, I can't stop to argue. I'm looking for a woman. A Mrs Baker. We've got her little boy in there and he wants his mum.' Rafferty pondered.

'Baker, Baker, Baker. Fair woman, stout?' Imogen shrugged.

'I haven't the faintest idea. But she must be around the thirty to forty mark.'

'That'll be her,' Rafferty said. 'Fractured femur, lacerated cheek, possible fracture left maxilla. Admitted Ward Ten five minutes ago. Come to think of it, she *was* asking about her little boy.'

Imogen decided to check before she told Michael. There was a phone in the lobby and she dialled Ward Ten. 'You've got him down there?' Sister said when she explained. 'Thank heaven. She's creating no end of fuss up here. I'll go and tell her we've found him and then I suggest he's admitted here. I can put him in a side ward with her. They can sort things out with Sister McFarlane in the morning.'

It seemed good sense to Imogen to reunite the little boy with his mother and Mr Wemyss agreed. 'Get him up there quickly, Nurse Brent, before the euphoria of the battlefield wears off. Ten to one that we'll be hauled over the coals tomorrow for admitting a child to that ward. And Sister McFarlane will be after my blood for farming out one of her precious children! However, "sufficient unto the day" etcetera.'

He crossed over to the little boy and gently

touched his cheek. 'There you are, Michael Baker. I told you we'd find your mum for you. You'll be with her in a couple of shakes. Nurse is going to take you up. Apparently she's been worried about you so she'll be glad to see you. All right?' The child nodded, smiling, and Imogen grasped the trolley to push him away. 'Let me help you,' Mr Wemyss said and together they turned the trolley around. At that moment Rafferty appeared.

'Was I right then, Nurse? Thought so. And this chap's for Ward Ten, is he?' He didn't wait for an answer and the next moment he was off, deftly threading the bulky trolley between the lines of wheelchairs and stretcher cases.

'Remind me to recommend friend Rafferty for Matron's equivalent of the VC,' Mr Wemyss said cheerfully and fell back to work. After what seemed like a lifetime a burly police sergeant came through the door, wiping his brow with a large handkerchief.

'That's that, then, folks!' We've ferried the rest of them to the District General so you've had your little lot for this night.' There was a murmur of relief from all sides and suddenly Imogen realised how weary she had become. She looked up at the clock and to her astonishment it showed half past eleven.

'Tired?' The tone was sympathetic and she turned to Mr Wemyss and nodded. 'A bit, sir. I suppose that's what it must be like in a war.'

He put out a hand and patted her arm. 'Well,

you behaved very well under fire, Nurse Brent. Considering it's your first time at battle stations you acquitted yourself very well.' Imogen saw his eye wander and turned to follow his gaze.

Sister Slater had just entered the Casualty Department, pushing a huge trolley filled with steaming cups. She was dressed in a tweed suit with a silk scarf tied over her head and had obviously been summoned from home to assist in the crisis. Mr Wemyss leaned towards Imogen and spoke in conspiratorial tones. 'Take good note of that, Nurse. I have a feeling it's the first and only time you'll see the Dragon acting as a tea lady.' Imogen smiled as she realised he had used Sister Slater's nickname. 'Wait till I tell Stella,' she thought and for the first time wondered what had become of her friend.

The last of the casualties was wheeled away to the ward. Ambulances arrived to take the others home and the staff gathered around the trolley for their cups of tea. You could almost hear everyone unwinding. The laughter was unnaturally loud, the voices slightly shrill. But everyone was proud of the way they had handled the incident. Imogen drank her tea and then went in search of Stella, desperate to get to her room and sleep.

'I'm going to sleep and sleep and sleep,' Stella said desperately but cheerfully. Her hair was straggling into her eyes and the top button of her dress was undone, but there was a look of satisfaction on her face. Imogen looked at her watch.

'*You* can sleep and sleep but I'm not sure about sleep and sleep and sleep,' she said. 'It's after midnight now and we'll have to get up at the usual time. We have to check whether or not we're needed again. We may not have tomorrow off at all.' Stella's theatrical groan echoed along the corridor.

'I've been working for Sister Frazer. I thought the Dragon was a slave-driver but she's Mary Poppins compared with Frazer! *Do this, do that, get this, get that, get a move on . . .*' As they walked along they swopped details of the patients who had passed through their hands. Apart from one man who had suffered a ruptured spleen and was in intensive care all the patients had a good prognosis.

'One way and another,' Stella said, 'it was a jolly good show. I wouldn't have believed we could all pull together like that, everyone mucking in and doing their bit. Even Rafferty. He was marvellous.' Imogen agreed.

'He was a jewel. Mr Wemyss thinks he ought to get the VC.' They were nearing the door to the nurses' home when Imogen heard the frenzied whisper behind her.

'Imo! Imo, hang on a moment. I've been trying to get hold of you all night.' She turned and saw Nicky. His face gleamed with sweat and his normally immaculate hair was tousled.

She heard Stella's impatient intake of breath behind her and turned.

'I'll go on, Imo. Don't be too long. Remember how late it is.' The next moment she had whisked through the door and Imogen turned back to Nicky. He moved nearer and grabbed her arm.

'Look, we haven't much time. If home sister catches me here at this time of night we've both had it. I've been out in the damned ambulances all night. I saw you once or twice, helping old Roger, and I tried to get a word with you but I couldn't. Where did you get to last night? I came over to dance with you again but you'd gone.' Imogen shrugged. 'Look,' Nicky said desperately, 'I'll pick you up tomorrow night, usual place. Say you'll come, Imo.' Imogen was struggling for words. 'Hurry up, Imo. I'll have to go.' She looked up into his impatient face, the brows down over the angry eyes. She put out a hand to the door.

'Goodnight Nicky,' she said firmly and passed through the door.

CHAPTER ELEVEN

'ARE YOU going home, Imo . . . if we're free, that is?' Imogen was still in bed when Stella poked her head around the door. She had been awake for hours and hours, her mind going round in circles, but there was still half an hour before they needed to report.

'I don't know,' she said. 'I can't really make up my mind until I know whether or not we're on duty. What about you?' Stella came further into the room and flopped on the end of Imogen's bed.

'I'm going home. As soon as I can get out of here. I'm lonely and forlorn and I need my mum. I'm going to weep on her shoulder and eat all her luscious meals and tell her what a marvellous son-in-law Clive will make.'

Imogen had mixed feelings about going home. It would be nice to be fussed over and she knew her parents would be pleased to see her but it would be impossible to put on a bright face for the whole weekend and if her smile slipped once her mother would be on to it in a flash. She couldn't face the thought of being questioned—about her love life or anything else. Stella offered to go and find out if they were needed and Imogen promised to make her mind up while Stella was away. She knew her friend was uneasy about leaving her alone for the weekend and when Stella came back to say they were not needed on the wards she made up her mind to tell a white lie.

'I'm going home after lunch,' she said firmly. 'I've got one or two things to do during the morning and I'm going to take things slowly. I had enough rushing yesterday. But you get away as soon as you can. I'll have lunch and then I'll catch the two o'clock bus.' Stella looked relieved and the two girls went down to breakfast.

They found everyone talking about the events of the night before. Each girl had a tale to tell. Of brave patients or ungrateful ones. Policemen who had helped and others who had hindered. The shocking way people used the motorway in fog and the tragedy of unused seat-belts. Everyone agreed Rafferty had been the star of the evening and that the staff as a whole had reacted well to a difficult situation.

'Sometimes,' Maria Valent said, licking in a stray bit of egg yolk, 'sometimes you wonder why you take up nursing. There must be easier ways of earning a living. And then something like last night happens and you know why you did it. You just know.' There was a murmur of agreement and then Stella made them all laugh with a recital of the sins of Sister Frazer.

The jobs Imogen had mentioned to Stella occupied the morning but the afternoon drag-

ged interminably. At one point Imogen almost
changed her mind and decided to go home
after all but in the end she fell asleep on her bed
and slept the sleep of exhaustion for more than
two hours. When she woke up she felt listless
and discontented. Her mouth was dry, her legs
heavy and she was bored. Even the paperbacks
on her bookshelf had ceased to attract and she
had no desire to join her fellow nurses in front
of the television. At six o'clock she could stand
it no longer. The late afternoon sun was lighting the dull red walls around the courtyard,
warming and softening where it fell. She decided to go for a long walk.

She took a quick shower and pulled on jeans
and a white mohair sweater. By the time she
got back it would be dark and there might be a
chill in the air. She pushed a pound note into
her pocket in case of emergencies and let herself quietly out of her room.

She was hardly outside the hospital gates
when she sensed that a car was drawing up
alongside her. With mounting horror she realised it was the dark green Volvo estate belonging to Mr Wemyss. It nosed ahead of her and
glided to a halt. The nearside door swung open
and she saw the surgeon's tall figure leaning
forward to look out.

'Imogen, please get in. I want to speak to
you. I've been hanging about for hours in the
hope that you'd come out.' She wanted to walk
on but her feet were refusing to obey her.

'Come on, get in. There's a good girl.' She could hear desperation creeping into his voice and she didn't blame him. They were right outside the hospital gates, in full view of the windows. Anyone could be looking out! She bent forward and looked into the car.

'I'm sorry. I've come out to get some fresh air. It's very kind of you to offer me a lift but I'd rather walk, if you don't mind.' To her annoyance her voice sounded weak and childish, her words stilted.

If she had expected Mr Wemyss to accept her refusal with good grace and drive on she was wrong. He switched off the engine of the car and leaped out. Before she could stop him he had seized her arms and was urging her into the passenger seat. When she resisted his grip tightened. 'Get in,' he said angrily and the next moment she was in the seat, the door was closed and he was coming round to take his place beside her.

'Where are we going?' she asked nervously as the engine roared to life.

'If I could trust myself I'd take you somewhere quiet and lonely where I could give you a piece of my mind,' he said grimly, never taking his eyes off the road. 'But as I appear to have taken leave of my senses and am no longer in command of myself I'm opting for a more civilised setting. There's a pub I know, a few miles out of town. They do a very good *coq au vin* there and their wine list is adequate. You, my girl, are going to sit across the table and talk to me. None of this dropping your eyes or turning away or hiding behind sister's skirts. We can't go on like this, Imogen. I almost called you Nurse Brent there, which shows you how mixed up I am. It's bad for discipline, bad for the smooth running of my clinic and what it's doing to my blood pressure God alone knows.'

Imogen sat for a moment while the houses petered out and gave way to open country. 'I can't go out for a meal,' she said eventually, trying to make her voice firm. 'I'm not dressed for eating out and I'm not hungry. And I'd be very grateful if you'd turn this car round and take me home!' His only reaction was a grunt of determination and she saw the needle of the speedometer flicker up to the speed limit.

'Did you hear what I said?' she cried indignantly, but before he could reply a low and rambling country inn loomed up in front of them and he swung the wheel to turn into the car park.

He got out and while he was coming round to open her door Imogen contemplated sitting tight in her seat and refusing to get out. But one look at his resolute face told her it would be useless. He was quite capable of lifting her bodily out of the seat and carrying her, kicking and struggling, into the hotel dining room. She got out with as much dignity as she could muster and put up a hand to smooth her hair.

'Don't fuss,' he said crisply. 'You look beautiful!' A few moments later she was sitting opposite him in a candle-lit room of enormous charm. At one end of the room a log fire sparked and crackled and brass fire-irons gleamed in the light. There was the smell of good food in the air and a low murmur of conversation from the other tables. In spite of herself Imogen began to relax and, seeing the strain leave her face, Roger Wemyss smiled.

'That's better,' he said. 'For a moment or two out there I was afraid you were going to defy me.' Imogen couldn't resist a smile of her own.

'What would you have done if I had?' she asked.

'Picked you up and carried you in by force,' he said at once.

'That's what I thought,' Imogen said drily and they both chuckled. She held up her glass. 'I suggest a truce,' she murmured. 'For one evening let there be perfect peace between us. I'm game if you are.' He clinked his glass with hers but shook his head.

'One evening is not enough, not nearly enough.' Imogen was glad when his eyes left her face and he picked up the menu. 'And now we must choose,' he said and held it out to her.

They began with a coarse pâté that melted on the tongue. 'I'm hungrier than I thought,' Imogen laughed as she spread still more pâté onto the tiny triangles of crisp toast.

'You're much too thin,' he said but there was such concern in his voice that Imogen could not take offence at his words. However, she couldn't resist a retort.

'I'm sorry I don't come up to your specifications,' she said primly but the look that flashed into his eyes at her words made her fall silent again. He would have spoken but at that moment the waiter arrived with the next course and Imogen busied herself with her plate.

The chicken was perfectly cooked, the vegetables crisp and succulent. She sipped the sparkling wine that filled her glass and wondered when they would get to the real purpose of the evening. She didn't have long to wait. After the *coq au vin* came strawberries and cream in frosted glasses and then a silver pot of coffee.

'Will you pour?' Roger asked and, as she raised the pot in trembling hands, he added, 'Try not to spill it, Nurse. I'd like to bring you here again and they're rather particular about their tablecloths.' She gave him an indignant glare that turned into a grin and went on pouring the coffee. As she raised the cup to her lips he began to speak.

'I don't know whether or not you realise it, Imogen, but for the past few weeks my clinic has been going to pot! No, don't look so alarmed. I'm not criticising your professional conduct or your nursing skills. It's nothing like that. But surely you can see that between us we've created a tense atmosphere. I don't know how it's affecting you but it's driving me up the wall! If I'm not careful I'll be making some disastrous medical error which will have me barred for life and I'm sure you don't want that to happen.' Imogen shook her head dumbly. He reached out and patted her hand.

'Cheer up. It's not as bad as that. What I'm going to suggest is that we try to get to know one another a little better. If we do, perhaps some of the tension will disappear. No, my dear girl, it's no use staring down at your plate. I know it's not easy to hear someone being as frank as this but I've come to the end of my tether. I've watched you mooning about in a daze over Fleming and I held my tongue. Now that you see him for what he is I think the time has come for me to speak. I want us to get to know one another, away from the hospital. And then perhaps we can get back to running my clinic as it should be run.'

Imogen looked up and met his eyes. They were blue and clear and full of kindness. How could she ever have seen this man as a cold, unfeeling brute? All the same, she was taken aback by his words.

'I don't know what to say,' she managed at last and wished she had said something more constructive. His hand was warm and firm and hers felt oddly at home inside it.

'Will you let me see you again?' he asked.

Imogen wanted to answer but the words would not come. It was too sudden. Only a day or so ago they had been nurse and surgeon, separated by a huge gulf of status and protocol. Now they were sitting together in candle light, he was holding her hand and she couldn't take it all in. From where she was sitting she could see the faint laughter lines around his eyes, the cleft in his chin, the way the fair hair grew crisp and curling around his ears.

'I don't know what to say,' she said desperately. 'I'm not being awkward, please believe me. And it's not that I wouldn't like to see you again, not at all. It's just—it's all a bit too much to take in. If you could give me time . . .' Her words tailed off as he squeezed her hand.

'Of course. There's all the time in the world. And now I'm going to pour you some coffee! Your hand shakes abominably. And when we've had coffee and a liqueur we'll talk about the ordinary mundane things of life and then I'll take you safely home.'

He was as good as his word. They drank coffee and sipped Cointreau and talked about food and wine and the world in general. His face lit up when Imogen told him about her dog, Benjie. 'He's a cross-bred Labrador,' she said. 'Terribly intelligent and affectionate. He's old now, almost thirteen, but I hope he's going to live forever and ever.' He nodded.

'I know what you mean. I have two dogs of my own. Retrievers. They're mother and daughter actually and I couldn't live without them. You'll love them too, I know that.'

He poured her another liqueur. 'That's the last one. There's a wild gleam coming in those eyes of yours and I think you've reached your limit. About the dogs, why don't you come over tomorrow and meet them? I could pick you up after breakfast and we could spend the whole day together. If you have no other plans, that is. If so, I shall demand that you break them.'

Imogen was still a little dumbstruck. 'I ought to go home tomorrow,' she said, 'but I could leave it till next week.' So the agreement was made. Roger would pick her up at the hospital gates at half past ten.

'Bring some comfortable shoes,' he said. 'We'll walk and walk and blow all the cobwebs out of our brains.' His hand was firm on her arm as he guided her back to the car and folded her into her seat. They spoke very little at first but as Lanchester came into sight Imogen took a deep breath and began. 'Thank you for a splendid evening,' she said formally. Roger inclined his head in thanks.

'The thanks are all mine, Imogen. It's been a relief to talk to you at last. I can't tell you what a relief.'

She felt she ought to say something, something sensible, and cleared her throat. 'I know I must have been difficult to work with lately,' she said, trying to keep her voice steady. 'I've been such an idiot . . . over Nicky and everything else. I promise you I'm going to pull up my socks!'

Suddenly the car was gliding to a halt and he was switching off the engine. The next moment his mouth came down on hers, so hard that when he drew it away she put up her hand expecting to find her lips were bruised. 'Sorry about that,' he said cheerfully as he switched on the engine and guided the car back onto the road. 'But you were talking such absolute rubbish that I couldn't think of any other way to shut you up.'

For the rest of the drive home Imogen sat silent and Roger made conversation out of the most trivial things. She wondered if he would kiss her again, when the car pulled up at the hospital gates. The very thought of such a thing caused her to shiver, with apprehension or pleasure, she couldn't be sure which. And then he was out of the car and coming round to hand her out. Their goodbyes were formal and a moment later she was hurrying through the gates towards the lighted hospital.

CHAPTER TWELVE

As soon as she woke up Imogen gave thanks that Stella had gone home for the weekend. There was no way she could have kept her agitation and confusion from her friend. Lying on her back, gazing at the peach coloured ceiling of her room, she thought over the amazing events of the last few days. If she hadn't known better she would have imagined it was all a dream.

She had never thought of Roger Wemyss as a man, let alone a lover. He was a distinguished surgeon, a figure of authority, her boss! She had never acknowledged the fact that he was a virile and attractive man. Until last night, and then it had dawned on her with a vengeance! She thought of him as he had followed her at the hospital gates, threatening to abduct her by force if she didn't get into the car. And then again in the car park of the inn. She giggled at the thought of what might have happened, seeing the tall figure striding into the dining-room with a girl in his arms—and a struggling girl at that! What a stir they would have made!

And then after, when she had decided to stay, he had been so nice, so considerate. Remembering the feel of his lips on hers she felt excitement swimming in her veins. She lay there, listening to her heart thudding in her ears, until a desire to see what the day would bring overcame her and she leaped out of bed.

While she cleaned her teeth she thought about Nicky, probing the wound to see if it still hurt. There was nothing. No pain, no anger, no sense of loss. When she closed her eyes she could hardly remember what he looked like. So much for infatuation!

She washed her hair and shook it free to dry and then made up her face with an absolute minimum of make-up. Deciding what to wear was difficult. In spite of the kindness Roger had shown her she was still a little in awe of him. She could imagine his home, a place of grace and elegance. What could she wear that would not look out of place? She settled for a slim skirt of soft blue Shetland tweed and matching sweater. There was a shawl to go with the skirt and she slung it over her shoulder, belting it in at the waist with a soft leather belt.

When she was ready she looked at herself in the mirror. The bright-eyed girl with the hectic flush who had run out to meet Nicky Fleming was gone. In her place stood a serene, clear-eyed woman. I look quite nice, Imogen thought and then put a hand to her face in confusion.

There was something she must do before she met Roger. Alexander Dodd was still in the ward and he would be expecting a visit. He was sitting up in bed when she got there, still playing with the toy soldiers Roger had given him.

'About time,' he said grumpily when he saw her but he was appeased when she explained about the disaster and all the extra work they had done. 'That still leaves yesterday,' he said. Without thinking she told him she had been out with Mr Wemyss and his face lit up. 'That's OK, then. Are you going to marry him? He's all right. In fact, I've decided he's going to be my doctor for good. *He* came in yesterday. *He* remembers.' The words were pointed but there was such an air of good humour about Alexander that they had no sting. It was hard to believe he was the same child who had caused such a furore the other day. So much for tomato sauce and toy soldiers, she thought as they made their goodbyes. Perhaps they should be available on prescription!

She was on her way downstairs when she saw Dr Graham coming towards her and as immaculate as ever. The fair hair was swept to the top of her head, there was the unobtrusive gleam of gold at her neck and her apple green dress clung to her splendid figure. Imogen was about to lower her eyes and pass discreetly by when Dr Graham hailed her.

'Good morning, Nurse Brent. You're off duty, I see. Well, you have a lovely day for it. I hope you enjoy it.' Imogen was still reeling with surprise when she reached the courtyard. If she hadn't known better she would have thought Dr Graham was drunk. It was the first time Imogen had heard her being pleasant to anyone but Mr Wemyss.

There was no sign of the green Volvo outside the gates and Imogen felt a sudden surge of disappointment. She turned her head to see if he was waiting further down the road and then she felt a hand on her arm. 'There you are. I'm parked over here. And we've got company.'

He was pointing towards a Range Rover parked at the kerb. There were two eager faces against the windows and Imogen squealed with delight when she saw them. 'They're lovely!' she cried and looked up to see a smile of pride on the stern face.

'Yes, they are rather nice,' he said, looking fondly at the dogs. 'But now we've got to subdue them so you can get in and sit down.' At last they had the dogs in the back seat and Imogen was installed beside him. As the Range Rover moved past the porters' lodge she caught a glimpse of Rafferty, open-mouthed at the window. Before they moved out of sight she saw that his astonishment had given way to a grin of sheer delight.

At that moment she felt a cold, wet muzzle press against her neck. 'And who are you?' she said, turning to the dog.

'That one's Babs,' Roger said, taking a quick

look sideways. There was something sheepish in his voice and Imogen looked at him sharply.

'Babs?' she said. 'That's a funny name for a dog.' He was staring at the road ahead but a guilty grin enveloped his face.

'Well, actually, I called her Baby when she was born and the name stuck. When I realised I couldn't go on calling a huge dog Baby she wouldn't answer to anything else and Babs was the best I could do. OK, go ahead and laugh.' Imogen tried to suppress a giggle.

'Well, it is hard to think of you calling a puppy Baby.'

'That's because you don't know much about me,' he said firmly. 'I quite often do things like that.' He turned the car in at a wide gateway and the wheels crunched on a gravel drive. She had expected a grand residence but the reality took her by surprise. The drive led up to a colonnaded porch and then swept on to an exit gate on the other side. The gardens in front of the house were delightfully informal but well tended.

The car pulled up at the door and he helped her out, the dogs tumbling after them. There were five white steps up to the door and they mounted them side by side. The hall was warm and welcoming with porcelain plates set on a high rack. The dull silk of Chinese rugs gleamed here and there on the parquet floor but the dogs skidded in their haste to get to a door on the far side.

'They smell roast pork,' Roger said. 'They're off to the kitchen for titbits.' But Imogen was fishing in her handbag.

'Here you are,' she said, producing a clean, white handkerchief. 'This belongs to you. Thank you very much for lending it to me.'

The dogs had no sooner vanished through the kitchen door than a motherly little woman appeared. 'This is Mrs Clyde,' Roger said. 'This is Imogen Brent, Mrs Clyde.' The woman smiled and nodded.

'It's nice to have you here, dear. I hope you're hungry. Lunch is nearly ready.' The smell of roast pork was reminding Imogen that she had never given a thought to breakfast. 'I'm famished,' she grimaced fervently and they all laughed.

Roger led her into the sitting room, a long, white-walled room with deep chairs and trailing houseplants here and there. Imogen recognised that the furniture was antique and valuable but there was nothing stiff or formal about the room. There was a log fire crackling at one end and they sank into easy chairs on either side. A decanter and glasses were set out on a low table and Roger began to pour.

'Would you like a dry sherry?' he asked. 'Or are you one of the modern brigade who prefer gin and tonic?' Imogen thought rapidly. Which would have the least effect on an empty stomach?

'Sherry would be fine, thank you,' she said at

last. Roger must have seen the doubt in her face. He handed her the glass and then looked at her sternly.

'Did you have any breakfast this morning? No, don't perjure yourself. No wonder you're so thin and those great eyes of yours seem to eat up your face.'

Imogen felt her cheeks flame. He made her sound like an Oxfam poster! The dogs came to her rescue, tumbling through the door licking their lips. 'I don't believe it,' Roger said sternly, looking down at them. 'You've been scrounging again. There's pork fat all round your whiskers.' He looked across at Imogen. 'Shall we take these reprobates into the garden and work some of the excess fat out of their systems?'

Imogen put down her glass and followed him through the french window into the garden. She couldn't resist letting out a little gasp of appreciation at what she saw. The garden seemed to roll on forever but the landscape was broken here and there by clumps of shrubs and small arbours.

They walked on, past a blazing pyracantha and borders planted with sweet smelling flowers and herbs. At last they came to rest in an arbour that dripped with white dog-roses. From here they could look back at the house and Roger described how he had found it, tumbledown and deserted, and restored it to its former glory. The sun gleamed back from the many windows, the walls glowing in the sun, and purple wisteria garlanded the lintel. 'It's heavenly,' Imogen said and meant that very word.

They stayed there, enjoying the scented air, until it was time to make their way back to the house and sit at the long refectory table. Mrs Clyde moved in and out, putting covered dishes on a heated trolley. When she was finished she said goodbye and vanished.

'She lives with her husband in the wing of the house,' Roger said. 'That's their domain and I never trespass. She leaves me in peace, except when she's taking care of me.'

While Roger carved the succulent pork Imogen helped them both to a selection of vegetables. 'What would you have eaten today in the home?' Roger asked, smiling.

'Nothing like this,' Imogen said and her tone was rueful. After that it was natural to talk about hospital and the people who worked there. They laughed over Rafferty and his constant fund of information. 'Misinformation most of the time,' Imogen said, 'but you've got to admit it's interesting!' Roger chuckled when she told him about her visit to Alexander Dodd that morning.

'That child will go far,' he said. 'Never mind his physical disabilities. Hopefully we'll have relieved them somewhat by the time he's adult. But any eight-year-old who can keep Celia Graham at bay has true grit. I've seen strong men quail in that situation, and I don't blame them.' Imogen had carefully avoided mentioning Dr Graham but Roger seemed quite happy to talk about her. 'I think I've had a lucky escape there.'

Imogen raised her eyebrows in question. 'Haven't you heard?' he went on. 'I've been replaced in her affections! There's a new consultant anaesthetist. He hasn't worked at the Royal before but on Friday he turned up to do a list. She liked the look of him and when he came back yesterday to clear up some of the motorway pile-up cases she looked on in theatre—and it was love at first sight for both of them! Well, second sight, but you know what I mean. They tell me he's a much better proposition than I ever was, more suitable in every way. I wish them joy of one another, that's all I can say.'

He was chuckling as he finished his tale but Imogen was remembering the glowing figure of the gynae registrar as she had seen her that morning. If that was what love did to you it was to be highly recommended. Roger was still talking, remembering the disastrous day in the clinic.

'I'll never forget your face when I pulled back that screen. You would willingly have died on the spot.' Imogen nodded.

'I was afraid the Dragon would swoop down on me.' Roger grinned sympathetically.

'You really have no need to fear Jean Slater,'

he said and there was an indulgent note in his voice. 'Her fiancé was killed in the war, at Arnhem. She was a nurse in training then so I'm told. Anyway, she decided to give her life to Lanchester Royal and that's what she's done. But she still remembers what it was like to love. She's known about you and I for some time, I'm quite sure of that. And she's given us a lot of leeway, you must admit that!' Imogen could barely comprehend the idea of Sister Slater as someone's fiancée but the more she thought about it the more possible it seemed. She had been indulgent to Stella when Clive came along and Roger was right when he said she'd given them a lot of leeway. Some of the emotions generated in the clinic this week must have communicated themselves to her and she had never said a word.

'I'll think of her more kindly in future,' Imogen said thoughtfully, 'and I'll try and persuade Stella to be less critical.' Roger smiled.

'Stella will make a good nurse eventually. I've seen her sort before. She's scatterbrained but her heart is in the right place. When she's given responsibility she'll measure up to it. I have no doubt about that.' Imogen glowed to hear him speak like that about her friend. She had always cared for Stella and it was nice to know Roger shared her opinion.

After the pork they had pears in wine and then carried their coffee through to the sitting room. 'Would you like some music?' Roger asked.

'What do you normally do after Sunday lunch?' she said. He looked a little guilty.

'Well, if you must know, I usually watch the cowboy series on TV. I know it's childish but I've never been able to resist a western, not since my schooldays.' Imogen settled in her chair.

'It's confession time,' she said. 'I adore westerns.' They sat for an hour while guns thundered and outlaws bit the dust. Imogen felt drowsy and contented. The fire was warm, the dogs lay sleeping at her feet, the man beside her was at peace. She tried to analyse her own feelings. She felt a new maturity within her. Was she falling in love with this man? If so it was a very gentle feeling, more satisfying than anything she had known with Nicky.

When the programme came to an end the dogs jerked upright, cocking their heads on one side and whining softly. 'They know it's time for their walk,' Roger said. 'Do you fancy getting some fresh air?'

They climbed into the Range Rover and headed for the distant hills. There was a faint chill in the air but the sun was shining and Imogen was glad she had chosen her skirt and shawl. They were warm and comfortable, clothes for enjoying the open air. Roger parked the Range Rover off the road on one of the foothills and they set their faces for the heights. Within a few minutes Imogen's cheeks were glowing, her skin tingling.

They walked in companionable silence, the dogs running ahead of them, until they were out on the open hillside. At last they sank down on the heather and looked down on the landscape below. Patchwork fields interspersed with tiny towns and villages looking as though they were made from a child's building bricks.

'It's beautiful, isn't it?' Imogen sighed and Roger nodded.

'The most beautiful country in the world,' he said. 'That's why I've never been tempted to leave it. I've had offers from abroad, very good offers on the whole, but this is where I belong.'

'Were you born here?' Imogen asked. He shook his head.

'I was born in Cornwall, just outside Penzance. My mother and sisters still live there. You'll love it. It's a strange and wonderful place but I've lived and worked here for the last ten years and I feel as though I've put down roots.'

As if he were afraid of the conversation becoming too intense he changed the subject. 'Tell me about your family,' he requested. She told him about her days at the bank. 'What a waste that would have been,' he said with conviction. 'You're a born nurse, Imogen. You do realise that, don't you?' His hand was lying on the heather only inches away from her own. She wished he would reach out and take it but he was staring into the middle distance. She had always been afraid of contact with Nicky, desiring it and fearing it at one and the same time, but now she wanted to feel this man's arms around her, holding her, crushing her! And if he did hold her she knew she would offer no resistance.

After a few moments he stood up, brushing sprigs of heather from his trouser legs. 'Time to go home,' he said, holding out a hand to pull her to her feet. They walked down the hill, the exhausted dogs padding behind. 'Are you ready for tea?' he asked as he let out the clutch. Imogen groaned.

'Have mercy. I'm too full from lunch.' But when she saw the tempting tea, laid out on the low table, she changed her mind. They toasted teacakes at the fire, holding them on long wire forks and then spreading them with butter and home-made strawberry jam. There were almond biscuits and tiny, triangular sandwiches and a pot of tea brewed from a kettle that sang in the hearth.

'Mrs Clyde will have gone home by now,' Roger replied when Imogen enquired where she was.

'I'd have liked to say goodbye to her,' Imogen said disappointedly, but a delicious quiver of excitement ran up her spine. They were alone!

After tea they fed the dogs in a gleaming copper clad kitchen and then settled down to put records on the stereo. 'The Mendelssohn Violin Concerto,' Imogen said happily as the notes filled the air.

'You know it?' Roger exclaimed in delight. They talked about music, finding their tastes were much the same. Imogen was sitting on the settee, her legs tucked underneath her, sensible shoes discarded on the floor. Roger sat opposite, the fair hair ruffled, the sleeves of his blue sweater pulled up to show muscular forearms. If she had dared Imogen would have crossed the divide and gone to him but twenty years of convention stopped her. The first move must come from him.

Her desire for him had grown almost unbearable when at last he levered himself to his feet and crossed to her side. 'Imogen,' he whispered. 'Oh, Imogen.' And then suddenly she was in his arms and his mouth was on hers, hard at first and then so gentle that it was like nothing she had ever known. She felt a tiny moment of fear and then she felt herself unfolding like a flower.

After a long moment he drew back his head and looked at her but she did not move or speak and he kissed her again. Slowly now and searchingly. When it came to an end she sighed deeply and leaned her head against his chest. She was afraid of the moment when they must look at one another and try to inject a note of reason into all this.

He put up a hand, so large that it could

cradle her head, and stroked her hair. 'My poor little Imogen. Don't look so confused. It's terribly simple really. I found that out a long time ago when I first realised how special you were becoming to me. I was confused then. I didn't know what to do so I ended up being hard on you. Please forgive me. I don't make a practice of that sort of thing, I can assure you.'

She tried to smile but her lips trembled. 'Don't be afraid, little Imo,' he said swiftly. 'You see, I even know your nickname. Don't be afraid. I won't do anything to frighten you, now or at any other time.' She wasn't afraid when his lips brushed her temple, not even when they lingered there. It felt so right that he should do it, so safe to be there beside him. If she'd dared she'd have put up a hand and run her fingers through his hair, allowed her own lips to trail gently across his cheek. She quivered and he smiled at her again, a reassuring smile.

'I'm sorry,' she said at last. 'I'm behaving in a terribly naive way. I promise you I'm not always so childish.' His grip on her tightened.

'Don't say that, my darling. It's that terrible innocence of yours that has reduced me to my present hapless state! I don't know whether or not you realise it, Imogen, but for the last few weeks I've been falling in love with you. No, don't shake your head like that. Let me finish. I don't know how it happened. I've worked with hundreds of nurses in my time and at least some of them were as beautiful as you. Lots of them were as capable as you. And none of them gave so much trouble! But somehow, in you, all the desirable qualities in a woman seem to come together. Perhaps I should blame it on pheromones. They're the things that get up your nose and set your senses ablaze—that's why you sometimes see the most unlikely people falling in love with one another.' Now at last she found words.

'Thank you very much, Mr Wemyss! I've often thought I got up your nose, now I know!' They both laughed and then Roger spoke again.

'I think I love you, Imogen. I think it's possible you love me a little although you may not realise it as yet.' Somehow Imogen found words.

'I think you're right. I know I feel strange . . . very strange. But very, very nice.' He would have kissed her then but she held up a restraining finger.

'Wait . . . let me go on. I thought I loved Nicky. I was burning up with love for him, or so I thought. But it burned out too quickly to be real love. Looking back I can hardly believe I was so foolish, so childish. Now, I feel quite different, almost serene. And very happy! Does that make sense?'

It was Roger's turn to be lost for words. Instead he shook his head as though astounded by the wonder of it all. Confidently Imogen moved into his arms, raising her lips to trace the line from jaw to ear. She felt a passion rising in him to match her own . . . and then he was drawing back.

'I think I'd better take you home. If you stay I won't be responsible for the outcome.' She opened her mouth to protest, to tell him that she would stay here forever if he asked her. But he was drawing her to her feet. 'Time to go home, little Imo. We'll be together tomorrow . . . and all the tomorrows.' Suddenly he grinned. 'And you can shut your mouth now, Nurse Brent. The time for astonishment is over!' The return to his old manner was too much for Imogen and she laughed and cried by turns.

'There'll be trouble when matron finds out,' she said, sniffing into his handkerchief.

'You leave matron to me,' he said. 'Besides, the Dragon will take care of you.' They walked together through the vast hall and down the steps, arms entwined, dogs weaving about their feet. And each of them knew they were walking towards a future of certain happiness.

4 Doctor Nurse Romances
FREE

Coping with the daily tragedies and ordeals of a busy hospital, and sharing the satisfaction of a difficult job well done, people find themselves unexpectedly drawn together. Mills & Boon Doctor Nurse Romances capture perfectly the excitement, the intrigue and the emotions of modern medicine, that so often lead to overwhelming and blissful love. By becoming a regular reader of Mills & Boon Doctor Nurse Romances you can enjoy EIGHT superb new titles every two months plus a whole range of special benefits: your very own personal membership card, a free newsletter packed with recipes, competitions, bargain book offers, plus big cash savings.

**AND an Introductory FREE GIFT for YOU.
Turn over the page for details.**

**Fill in and send this coupon back today
and we'll send you
4 Introductory
Doctor Nurse Romances yours to keep**

FREE

At the same time we will reserve a
subscription to Mills & Boon
Doctor Nurse Romances for you. Every
two months you will receive the latest
8 new titles, delivered direct to your door.
You don't pay extra for delivery. Postage and
packing is always completely Free.
There is no obligation or commitment –
you receive books only for
as long as you want to.

It's easy! Fill in the coupon below and return it to
**MILLS & BOON READER SERVICE, FREEPOST, P.O. BOX 236,
CROYDON, SURREY CR9 9EL.**

Please note: **READERS IN SOUTH AFRICA** write to
Mills & Boon Ltd., Postbag X3010,
Randburg 2125, S. Africa.

FREE BOOKS CERTIFICATE

**To: Mills & Boon Reader Service, FREEPOST, P.O. Box 236,
Croydon, Surrey CR9 9EL.**

Please send me, free and without obligation, four Dr. Nurse Romances, and reserve a
Reader Service Subscription for me. If I decide to subscribe I shall receive, following my free
parcel of books, eight new Dr. Nurse Romances every two months for £8.00, post and
packing free. If I decide not to subscribe, I shall write to you within 10 days. The free books
are mine to keep in any case. I understand that I may cancel my subscription at any time
simply by writing to you. I am over 18 years of age.
Please write in BLOCK CAPITALS.

Name _____

Address _____

_____

_____ Postcode _____

SEND NO MONEY — TAKE NO RISKS

*Remember, postcodes speed delivery. Offer applies in UK only and is not valid to
present subscribers. Mills & Boon reserve the right to exercise discretion
in granting membership. If price changes are necessary you will be noti-
fied. Offer expires 31st December 1984.*

8DN

EP11